PRAISE FOR BILL RANSOM

"A novel of vampire seduction, murder, intrigue, and blood. Accomplished poet and novelist Bill Ransom uses humor in especially delicious ways."

—Brian Herbert, New York Times bestselling coauthor of *Dune: House Atreides*

"Brother Blood, Sister Death is a classic vampire novel rife with secrets ... but it's no secret that I loved it! Complicated relationships and unexpected twists and turns mix with good old-fashioned vampire violence for a great read. More, Bill Ransom!"

—Nancy Holder, New York Times bestselling coauthor of the Wicked Series

"Brother Blood, Sister Death is a highly entertaining, riveting story about twin adult vampires. Daniel and Diana struggle to live in the human world, but Diana's appetite for killings goes beyond survival. Daniel worries about his own safety, and things become bloody twisted. Couldn't put this one down—definitely worth a bite."

—Anna Quinn, author of *The Night Child* (Psychological Thriller, Blackstone, 2018)

BROTHER BLOOD SISTER DEATH

BILL RANSOM

WFP
WORDFIRE PRESS

EBook ISBN: 978-1-68057-017-5
Trade Paperback ISBN: 978-1-68057-019-9
Hardcover ISBN: 978-1-68057-016-8

Cover design by Janet McDonald
Cover artwork images by Adobe Image
Kevin J. Anderson, Art Director

Published by
WordFire Press, LLC
PO Box 1840
Monument CO 80132

Kevin J. Anderson & Rebecca Moesta, Publishers

WordFire Press eBook Edition 2020
WordFire Press Trade Paperback Edition 2020
WordFire Press Hardcover Edition 2020
Printed in the USA
Join our WordFire Press Readers Group for
sneak previews, updates, new projects, and giveaways.
Sign up at wordfirepress.com

❀ Created with Vellum

DEDICATION

Thanks to:
Maud Ransom
Annie Marcoe
LaVerne Ransom
Who taught me to read.
Ms. Joanne Baird
Who taught me to type.

CHAPTER ONE

S he'd kept only one secret from her twin brother, and she intended to keep keeping it, but she'd have to confess tonight's disaster. She had to stop the wrong because she couldn't make it right. She rode beside their Proxy in his leather-plush Lincoln Navigator. Payment for their clandestine needs had bought the Proxy this wallowing whale of a car. He knew most of their accounts, had produced their last two sets of IDs; then he initiated a relationship with her that was forbidden, dangerous, unforgivable. He was arrogant in this betrayal of her brother, unexciting in bed, the kind of man who lied about a vasectomy. He switched on a satellite channel that doled out fake jazz for B-movie seductions, and she rolled her eyes.

"Pull in over here," she said, and pointed out the turnoff to a small county park just off the road beside a stream. She touched her mother's ivory-handled penknife, secure inside her calf-high ostrich leather boot, and stepped out of the car before it lurched to a stop. She hurried behind a grove of vine maples to a picnic table overgrown by blackberries, out of the headlights of the few passing cars.

"For someone who wanted to talk you were pretty damn quiet in the car," he said. He approached with a swagger, like he was in charge. "What's up?"

"I was pregnant," she said.

"*Was?* You said you couldn't ... that you'd never even had a period—"

She snatched his trachea with an eagle claw grip, and wrestled him,

1

fish-eyed, gape-mouthed to the ground. His hands scrabbled at her hands and tore at her hair.

"It was a *thing*," she snapped, and squeezed harder. He thrashed and bucked and squirmed into the blackberries. "Eating its own placenta!"

She was out of shape, two months without her personal gym, no long night runs for weeks. He clawed at her hands, tripped her, and rolled both of them up in blackberry vines. Better leverage on her two-handed grip turned his crunched trachea into a sock full of wet cotton. The Green Beret who'd taught her that grip was the only man she'd fucked whom she hadn't killed. She was grateful for the grip; it was the least she could do.

The Proxy's body went limp, his lights out, but she held firm for a moment. She released one hand to slip her mother's ivory-handled knife from its sheath in her right boot.

"I betrayed my brother for *you*," she snarled. As soon as it was out, she knew it wasn't true. She'd betrayed her brother for the thrill, to see how close she could get to the edge of what held them together. She had to make a wrong thing right.

She nicked his carotid with her mother's knife, then wrapped her legs around him and sucked down all she could before she got too full and too woozy to drive. Her missed step on the slippery slope between thrill and death had killed the Proxy, and now she couldn't remember whether she'd *meant* to kill the Proxy or whether she'd just *happened* to kill the Proxy.

Slipping, she thought. *Slip slip slipping*.

She'd begun to share her brother's concern about her mental ... differences. She took a moment to catch her breath and to steady herself from the inevitable onslaught of a recent, disturbing change—disorientation, dissociation ... *confusion*.

She dragged the Empty the few yards to a small stream and washed off the obvious from both of them. They'd only be in the car for half an hour, no moon, little traffic, tinted windows. She dragged him back to the passenger side, then grunted and cursed as she wrestled him up and into the seat. Two months without her weight set was starting to show. She climbed into the driver's seat, tilted the rearview mirror, and saw the hatchwork of scratches on her forehead and hand, one fingernail puncture next to her right eye.

"You nearly got it," she said, and patted the Empty's thigh. "Nice try. Wouldn't have helped."

Headlights in the mirror cast a silver sheen across her wild tangle of hair, flecked with bits of brush and dead leaves. No serious damage. Blood down the front of her northwest-gray Vergara suit. She'd rushed the payoff and made herself too woozy now to think or to care. She belted her Empty into the passenger seat, leaned his seat back, and pulled his jacket up to his chin. Her matching shoulder bag at his feet held her brother's tactical tools. She hefted the bag and dropped it.

Yep, guess I meant to. She fastened her seat belt and patted her Empty's cheek. "Gotta go." She'd need those tools when she got to their storage unit.

The Empty's Lincoln was a boat, a barge that wallowed out of the little roadside park and onto the highway back to the city. She reviewed the details of the identity on her two-month-old license in case she was pulled over. Soon she would be in no condition to dredge up memories of any kind.

Tomorrow will be a new ID, new details, new "narrative."

Her brother loved that word, "narrative." She preferred "story." He would be prepared, but angry, their backup ID already safe in his old puzzle-box. A scramble of gravel under the tires startled her back onto the highway, heart racing.

Too close!

She'd already wasted too much time on the Empty, her brother's so-called ultra-secure (he preferred "uber-secure") Proxy.

Proxy Rule number one: no face-to-face contact. Rule number two: do only what is agreed upon. Rule number three: only strategic, logistic, or tactical questions.

Breaking any of the three rules turned a Proxy into an Empty, usually her brother's job. This Proxy managed a perfect three.

She told the Empty beside her, "You forced me into an executive decision."

She stuck the Empty's thumb drive into the console but it only played "How to get ahead in the insurance business" lectures and affirmation mantras. Late-night radio brought the full spectrum of Christian music and sermons, backed up with the alien-obsessed DJ in Pahrump, Nevada, that her brother liked. Which of her own music would she play if she had it? "Sympathy for the Devil?" "Stairway to Heaven?"

Definitely "Stairway to Heaven." She'd even named her favorite plant "Robert."

She switched off the radio-babble because she caught herself drifting out of her lane again. Memories unspooled, her life chained to one after another of her brother's Proxies, a blur of code names, most without faces. This one had bypassed her brother "to talk over coffee" when he knew in-person contact was forbidden. His intentions were neither talk nor coffee but betrayal and money and sex. Their relationship ended in this slash and quiver of impotent wrestling in that small county park outside Portland. Her brother should be grateful she was cleaning this one up herself.

The Proxy'd been right about her lack of periods. Her brother claimed their kind were hybrids, infertile mules, but he still ordered condoms for his women "in case it's a virus." She didn't like sex with men anyway, but she liked how they always fell for it. The bitterness of testosterone spoiled the payoff. She wished she could stick to estrogen, but hungry beggars couldn't be choosey.

She hated driving because of the crippling headlights, fear of getting pulled over, fake ID, questions. Maybe delay, detainment, death. Dark glasses didn't help. When full, she got dizzy and disoriented around lights and movement and questions. She couldn't always remember which *she* she was supposed to be, but she knew better than to risk being detained until daylight. She would wake up from this with her new ID on her pillow and her brother starting the whole grind over. She couldn't stay conscious much longer. She wanted to be done with the Empty and back home in her bed before daylight. Her beautiful bed beside Robert, her beautiful plant, in their drab drab apartment in their drab drab building in their gritty, gray neighborhood by the river.

Brother will be pissed.

Brother never moved without force even if he wanted to move.

Plan plan plan and think think think but no move move move.

She snapped alert when she almost missed the port exit and slid the Empty's Lincoln sideways down the curve. He slumped onto her shoulder and she shrugged him upright at the stop sign. No traffic. She patted her Empty's cheek.

Now maybe Brother will get us out of here.

She rounded a dumpster in the alley behind their warehouse storage and crunched the front bumper against a fire hydrant. She only wanted to sleep and was not tracking well, but she had to complete her mission, wobbly or not. 4:00 AM, no traffic, no cameras. She pulled the storage key from the slit inside her belt and was glad she didn't have to remember a code.

Brother loves his codes.

She yanked open the roll-up door to access their white, thirty-foot box van and immediately banged her shin on the tow unit linked to their Mercedes wagon. She'd wanted red but Brother said, "No! Too much attention!", so she got ugly suburban tan.

She missed attention. The Proxy had given her attention. She dragged the body out of its car and stumbled over the tow unit again. The Empty broke her fall, and she struggled to untangle herself from its unwieldy weight. She grunted it into the van, then rolled it into her twin's chest freezer atop their emergency food and Brother's lab supplies. She scrambled back to the Lincoln for the tools to finish the job.

She drove exhausted and afraid. Locked the Proxy's car outside their apartment, left the keys for Brother's disposal through their new Proxy. Brother always had a Proxy-in-waiting and a stack of extra IDs in his old puzzle-box. She dreaded learning new IDs.

She didn't remember driving home, but she beat the sunrise and beat her brother home from work. She spit a dribble of blood into one large, bruise-purple leaf-trap on Robert the flytrap, tickled it with her finger-nail to watch it close.

"G'night, Robert," she said. She atomized a mist of distilled water and puffed a lungful of CO_2 at the plant. She flopped onto her bed, her jacket and blouse bloodied, just in time to embrace the onslaught of her three-day torpor.

Her final thought before darkness: *Two months in this hole! Now he'll have to fix it. Now we'll get the hell out of here.*

CHAPTER TWO

He closed and re-taped the door to his makeshift clean room, then downloaded identity details and property information from his new Proxy, Darkest Knight, into his double-encrypted laptop. Now they were Daniel and Diana Cazador. He repeated the names several times and marveled at the likenesses in their new passports. Pachelbel's "Canon in D" on guitar filled his headphones, and he nodded to the rhythm. He viewed his screen through dark glasses and a clown ski mask. Red lighting and red paint on the walls eased the itch on his eyes. He could use the computer's voice feature, but he preferred music. He didn't want his sister to hear anything about their new Proxy. Her recent lapse in judgment had launched them into retreat, safe mode, new identities. Daniel knew his job was on the line, a job he'd managed well for two months. It allowed them to survive and to lay low. But they'd squeaked by too long this time, and with too much sacrifice. His twin's lack of self-control escalated by the week. Now her selfishness had cost them a Proxy, their current identities and the backup identities arranged by the Proxy. Truly anonymous Proxies who fit their needs were hard to find, even through the dark web.

And now we have a dead guy in my freezer and an untested Proxy with a dramatic flair. "Darkest Knight," my ass!

Their new contractor's test run began with disposal of the dead Proxy's Lincoln, photoreconnaissance of their new property up north, and rental of a new private, secure warehouse storage. Through internet contact and money transfer he'd purchased an unfinished house on a bluff before they had to go dark this time. Now he'd have to finish the work himself that he'd wanted to hire out from a distance.

Daniel's present clean room was a dark, hot, and humid closet lined with four layers of aluminum foil and aluminum tape, nowhere near the copper mesh clean room he'd installed in their San Francisco home. That home was now very expensive rubble on a prime hillside lot overlooking the San Francisco Bay. His sister's indiscretions forced their move to Portland and this decline in creature comforts in their ratty apartment overlooking the river. New sheets of copper mesh for their next clean room lined the interior of their box truck holding the Empty and most of their immediate needs—tools, lab equipment, electronics, a made-up bed for emergencies. After work, he'd use a Puerto Rico IP address to summon furniture and their other large items from POD storage in Mendocino, California and Chimayo, New Mexico to Washington state.

Diana secured their new passports and drivers' licenses with his puzzle-box just before she violated security rule #1: Never meet the Proxy in person. Daniel had spent his free time for the past three days repeating his new name, "Daniel Cazador," and Daniel Cazador's life narrative over and over. He readied their immediate belongings for a nighttime bug out. He used their same birthdays to make the ID switch easier on his twin but changed the year as needed. She hated the change, even when she caused it. They would have to perfect an adjusted family narrative immediately.

I have the plan to save us both—permanently. Just one more month to perfect it ... and she just couldn't wait.

She'd begun to unravel in San Francisco like a common junkie, her incidents coming closer and closer together, more and more indiscreet, to the point of photos in the *Chronicle* and attention from that DJ in Pahrump about new cases of "spontaneous human combustion."

Darkest Knight uploaded floor plans and new photos of their house. Daniel had bought the two-story Victorian knock-off at a county auction up in northern Washington. The original owners, from San Francisco, had disappeared. No next of kin and no bodies, so the legal nightmare was handled remarkably fast by a bank that only wanted money. Daniel's last Proxy had negotiated a very good price. The house itself was basically complete except for their appointments, paint, and furnishings. Their attached garage was framed up with a roof and utilities but no exterior walls. Daniel had hoped to have it completed before Diana forced another move. Now they wouldn't have the time to wait, and another interim hideout was impractical. Lately her appetite had forced him into some stupid moves of his own.

A co-worker at Harbor Hospital had a supervisor searching lunch-boxes, so Daniel planned to quit tonight and make the move. He'd wanted another month to build up provisions and to contract the job for the garage exterior. Lately his sister's patience shortened and her anger smoldered more every day. She'd already spent her first waking day in her room, not memorizing her new ID, "Diana Cazador."

Daniel called up the satellite photos of their Washington property and said, "Bigger." The gray on gray on gray speck on his screen enlarged to a sprawling community at the northernmost tip of a peninsula on a peninsula. A two-lane road separated cranberry bogs on one side from the Strait of Juan de Fuca and Canadian islands on the other. The Strait, the road, the roofs on the buildings and the sky oozed gray. Sand dunes, gravel driveways, budding alders and willows all framed the blood-red cranberry bogs in that somber, gray veil. A tongue of white fog licked at the red heart of the bog.

He homed in on the house and their twenty wooded acres right on the bluff and hoped that storms off the Strait wouldn't send driftwood through the picture windows. In the daytime that could be a disaster. He made a notation on the photo: "Rigid blackout blinds?"

He printed a hard copy for Diana.

Portland's closing in on her. On us.

She'd blundered into a dark and reckless desperation. He'd blundered into carelessness at the hospital. Twice the shift supervisor had double-checked inventory in the cooler behind him, always a bad sign. A rural move meant more limits on Diana. His twin's special needs and expensive tastes kept their catastrophe bags packed while Daniel negotiated their next safe place. His technical expertise slipped them past lawmen and others who lately employed shiny new tools of their own.

We have to end these flights-in-the-night!

He printed out the website photos of the house's interior, much more important to Diana than the beautiful stand of trees. High ceilings, open floor plan with two bedrooms, each bigger than the apartment they now shared, each with a bathroom and an adjoining office, fully wired. The large living room and dining room presented a fresh gallery for their art collection, too long in storage. The kitchen was small, but only Daniel was interested in cooking. Walls glared flat white latex that Diana wouldn't abide for long.

Good. Get her painting instead of pouting.

The tingle from his computer monitor morphed into itchy eyes and cheeks, the backs of his hands. He switched off his machine and told himself, "Don't rub!" He'd lasted almost an hour at the screen this time, and believed he'd made progress.

It works on kids with peanut allergies.

He took off his face protection and left his clean room. A string of red LEDs illuminated the living room just enough and immediately relaxed his eyestrain. The combination of flickering fluorescents and intense incandescents at work was torture already; he didn't need advanced aggravation. He set the property photo onto his TV tray for Diana and circled a large, partly-skeletal blob of a building at the north-ernmost margin.

Daniel had paid their dead Proxy to buy the building at a tax auction. They couldn't accumulate *things* over the years, except what they'd abandoned in POD storage under different names from Chimayo to Chico. But they did have *money*. Multiple bank accounts languished in seven states and two Canadian provinces; so many identities now that he kept a logbook with his cedar puzzle-box of extra passports. Diana wanted *things* again, so he'd dangle *things* to fill their new house.

"If I'm spending my life in prison, then I want a nice one," she'd said, and agreed to the deal.

"Cazador," he said, then repeated, "Cazador." He liked the feel of the new name on his tongue, strong with an air of mystery. He riffled the pages of their new passports, one set Canadian, and admired his new Washington State driver's license with its "enhanced" ID, good for Canada, just in case. He would have to refit the truck in case of a run to Canada. He never knew who took these exams for him, but exams—real or hacked—and insertion of their likenesses onto passports and other ID cost ten thousand dollars. The Proxy took care of their stand-ins. Once out of Portland and up in Washington, Daniel would deal with his new Proxy, self-proclaimed "Darkest Knight," always a great risk.

Getting a new Proxy is riskier, pricier, he cautioned himself. *Especially in the boonies.*

Dark drapes and electrical tape squeezed the last of the sunset out of their living room, and three blasts from the riverfront ferry warned Daniel he had less than an hour before his shift at Harbor Hospital a mile away.

One way or another, my last shift.

Diana had slept for three days, and Daniel's anger kept her pouting in her room for the rest of the week while he fine-tuned an exit from their situation. His gaze took in their living and kitchen area: bare, off-white walls and slate-gray linoleum tiles peeling back from their edges at the floor. Moving cartons and two large backpacks lined up against the wall. Wooden TV trays and fold-up chairs. Their extensive collection of Japanese paintings remained unpacked in their white, unmarked box truck alongside his tools and lab gear and the dead Proxy in their freezer.

Daniel's new custom-made appliance with polished stainless steel sat atop a second TV tray. His best work, this fresh drink dispenser, waited with a clean martini glass under a serpentine stainless spout. Their new, real lives awaited. He let out a tense breath and pushed the recurring image of the frozen Empty out of his mind.

He must've been a helluva talker, Daniel thought, and shook his head. *Not much of a thinker.*

Diana slammed the bathroom door in her bedroom, his cue to prepare the drink that should last her through his shift. He placed a two-fisted pink glob of dough-like material he'd dubbed "Matrix" into the hopper atop his drink dispenser. She was not happy with her new name, nor that this time the new name and everything that would follow was their shared fault.

"Bloody Mary," he said. A low, vibrating hum swallowed the Matrix down and drizzled out a perfect serving. The other side of the machine extruded a coil of gray paste.

"Shouldn't be a martini glass," he grumbled. "But that's how she wants it." He finger-wiped a hesitant drop from the lip of the spout and took a critical taste.

She'll say it's too bland, he thought. *She'll say Matrix sucks out the spice.*

She'd been ungrateful, edgy, and dangerous for these few months she'd had to keep to her room, waiting for a new safe house and for his perfection of Matrix and its appliance. She couldn't be trusted alone, though he had to trust her, even now. Two moves ago, he'd given up locking her bedroom door when she'd burst through it one night to prove a point. Their situation required trust, and anger burned up energy he couldn't afford. Neither could afford real trouble with the other, twins forever linked by their unique malady.

Might as well be Siamese twins sharing a heart, he thought.

While he waited for Diana to dress, he rolled up his sleeves, slathered SPF 50 sunscreen onto his arms and face, then slipped on his sunglasses and peeled back a crack in the drapes. He held his trembling hands into a last triangle of sunset for the few quick breaths it took for hives to crawl up his arms and across his face. He taped the drapes shut tight when he heard the bedroom door handle *click.*

Diana took a tentative step into the room, her head and shoulders swathed in blue silk scarves atop a white, slinky cocktail dress by Lauren, her most treasured *thing* that she refused to pack. The breath she'd been holding came out in a long *hisss.*

Daniel tossed her a new passport, and she let it bounce off her chest onto the floor.

"You're Diana Cazador now," he said. "Practice this time."

She ran a trembling finger down his greasy arm and said, "You're crazy. You can't make yourself one of *them.* Why do you even *want* to?"

"You should be grateful that I get as close as I do. You keep us on the run. I keep us alive."

Diana stalked around the TV table, her gaze focused on the drink he'd prepared.

She swept an arm to take in their drab, nearly empty apartment. "You call this 'living'?" she asked.

"I call it 'alive,'" he said.

"This time it's *your* fault!" she snapped, her voice petulant as a two-year-old's. She sat on the corner of a packing box, faced her drink at eye-level, peeled off her extra layers of scarves and dropped them to the floor. Both hands gripped her knees.

"I got careless at work because you couldn't manage your intake," he countered. "Which came first?"

Daniel set his sunglasses aside and toweled off his sunscreen.

"That crap you invented just doesn't make it for me," she said, still fixated on the glass. "I'm dying here."

"It gets us by," he said, "and I have a plan."

"Uh-huh. Beauty parlors. So you can get laid while I 'get by.' I thought you said that 'phlebotomist' was the Plan of plans."

He tossed his towel at her but hit the TV tray. Her reflexes snatched up the martini glass without a drop lost. She sucked down her drink and licked the glass.

Daniel pulled on a long lab coat with "Harbor Hospital" stitched above the pocket. His ID tag read:

Hunter, Darius

Phlebotomy

He flicked a finger against the tag and said, "Remember, after tonight, no more 'Darius,' no more 'Dolores.' We're Daniel and Diana. Practice." His phone pinged an alert that his Uber driver waited outside.

Diana's eyes closed, and she swayed on her perch like a slender, pale bird.

"Hey!" he snapped, and shook a finger at her. "You hold off till I get back. I'll bring you something straight from work."

Diana growled, "Next time you shake a finger at me, Brother Dear, I'll bite that fucker off!"

He checked his watch, chanced a glimpse through the drapes to be sure that the sun was down. He put on his hat, overcoat and black goatskin gloves, snatched up his leather briefcase and slammed the door behind him without a glance back.

CHAPTER THREE

D aniel stepped out of the driver's warm, black Soul and snugged his coat tighter against the cold and damp. His good Italian shoes splat-splatted through the parking lot puddles. His briefcase held two roast beef sandwiches and Stephenie Meyer's novel *Twilight*. Diana thought it amusing. Daniel couldn't finish it.

A bored security guard checked Daniel's ID, opened and closed the briefcase. He held up the book and said, "My wife wants to read this. Any good?"

"My sister liked it."

"What about you?"

"Not my kind of thing," Daniel said. "Give it to your wife with my regards."

The guard thanked him more than the book deserved and motioned him through Harbor Hospital's ER entrance.

Daniel hung up his coat and hat in the supply room, then plopped his briefcase onto the counter. He noted his co-worker Lou's interest in the briefcase, but conversation was limited to floor and patient assignments for the night. He was sure this snoop was the one who got yesterday's day shift's lunch boxes and backpacks checked on the way out. Daniel quietly filled his cart with cooler, glassware, IV sets, and syringes to make his first set of rounds.

The comatose young marathoner in Trauma Care ICU bequeathed him a unit of O neg that Daniel stashed beneath his rack of blood draws.

Lou met up with Daniel in the lab for their first break and to unload their carts. They set vials with different colored caps into racks with matching colors. Lou wore a new lapel button that said, "The Vampire is in!" Daniel opened a gray-top vial and sniffed the contents.

"Hep C for sure," Daniel said. "Inactive herpes." He added a blank label under the patient's name and placed it into its rack. "Wanna bet?" he asked.

Lou shook his head and didn't meet Daniel's gaze. "No, man," he said. "I lost to you three times last night. I'm a believer." He crossed to the coffeepot to pour himself a cup and again showed interest in Daniel's briefcase over the coat rack. "That looks expensive," he said. "Real leather?" He felt the pebbled exterior, examined the clasp.

"Ostrich," Daniel said. He walked over to the briefcase, opened it wide enough that Lou couldn't help seeing inside, and pulled out a sandwich.

"I can't believe you eat in here," Lou said, with a head shake. "Some days I'm nervous just drinking coffee in here." He took a sip and turned to point at their carts. "Think about what's in all that glassware. Viruses. Spirochetes. Jesus!"

Daniel couldn't help himself. Through a mouthful of roast beef on rye he asked, deadpan, "Jesus in the glassware?"

"No, no. Viruses and spirochetes in the glassware. 'Jesus' for emphasis." He pointed to Daniel's sandwich and made a face. "Do you cook that roast beef at all? Godawful bloody mess!"

Lou was the most humorless person at Harbor Hospital, in Daniel's experience. Also, the nosiest about co-workers' personal lives. While focusing on the briefcase, he hadn't seen Daniel toss back the contents of an extra purple-top he'd drawn.

As if reading Daniel's mind, Lou asked, "Hey, when do I get to meet that mysterious sister of yours? She seeing anybody?"

"I'd love to introduce you, Lou. How about tomorrow after work?"

Lou shook his head. "Off tomorrow," he said. "Visiting my parents in Tualatin for their anniversary. How about Saturday? Does she like to dance?"

Daniel took the last bite of his sandwich, tossed the wrapper into the garbage and brushed crumbs off his lab coat. "She loves to dance," he said. "And wrestle. Saturday's perfect."

Lou perked up. "Wrestle? Really?"

Daniel invented an address and phone number, then wrote it on one of the labels and handed it to Lou.

"Wow, Hunter, thanks! I thought you didn't like me."

Daniel almost slipped to correct his name: "Cazador," his new ticket to freedom.

Darius Hunter's dead in a couple of hours, he thought.

Daniel clapped Lou on the shoulder. "It's not that I don't like you," he said. "Just don't know you." He pushed his cart to the door. "Here we go for round two." He had to hurry to lift another unit from the abdominal cramping in 206 before the floor nurse got there.

CHAPTER FOUR

Diana pulled her black tailored greatcoat over her black double-silk tunic and black silk bell-bottoms with quick-release cinch that rode just above the crack in her butt. No bra, no nothing else, just a black watch cap that secured her cascade of strawberry blonde hair. She loved the way silk exaggerated the sensual intimacies of the world, even the cool nip of a lewd Portland breeze. The pockets of her greatcoat held a pint of hundred-proof vodka, a lighter and three fat joints.

Dressed for success, she thought. Her brother would say, "Dressed for disaster."

He'd come home with his Matrix crap, but she had the need, she had the wants, and she knew tonight, after only a week, would mean more trouble with *Brother.*

Trouble trouble trouble.

She sniffed the breeze and an electric tingle coursed from her core to her fingertips, toes, skull, lips, tongue.

Teeth.

She ran her tongue along the edges of those perfect teeth that she learned long ago rendered her perfect smile as captivating as her piercing, green-eyed gaze.

Every predator works to her strengths.

Another sniff and Diana followed her nose down Sam Jackson Parkway to the Marquam Nature Park shelter. After the last evening bus, homeless teens and wanna-be-homeless suburban Goth types gathered at the shelter to score what could be scored or to sell what could be sold, then scurried up the trail for privacy. She wanted a girl, this time. Boys were easier, just not as satisfying. The Proxy was a complete waste, she had to admit that now.

Four boys and two girls, all dressed in anarchist black, started up the trail. A short girl with a butch haircut and a cigarillo between her teeth came back to Diana and asked her for a light.

"Well," Diana said, "I don't smoke ... *those*. They'll kill you, but they don't say when." Flash of a smile. She pulled a joint and lighter from her pocket and said, "How about we try *this*?"

"All *right*!" the girl said. She slipped the cigarillo into her shirt pocket and accepted the joint. The others had already wandered out of sight.

Diana lit the joint for her and kept the girl's gaze until she lost it through a coughing fit. Her gaze always worked on girls eventually, gay or not. Gay girls found her body as interesting as the boys did, so the gaze was just punctuation on the sentence. Non-gay girls thought that she might attract some not-gay guys. The girl handed back the joint, patted her substantial chest as though apologizing for the cough, and met Diana's gaze immediately. The joint did nothing for Diana, but she took her turn anyway.

"Do you have anything to drink?" the girl asked. "I'm really more of a juicer." Even so, she took back the joint and gave it a big pull.

"I do," Diana said, "but I don't have anything here to mix it with." She'd learned patience long ago. *Don't hurry them. Wait until it's their idea.* Offering too much too soon set off alarms in street kids.

"Whatcha got?"

The joint came back, and Diana faked it again, slowly this time, holding that gaze.

"Vodka, hundred-mile, a little harsh to take it straight." Diana showed her the bottle. "You're welcome to give it a go."

The girl uncapped the bottle and sipped some off the top. She shuddered.

"Whooo! That's pretty dank stuff! Whadda *you* drink it with?" She handed back the bottle and took the joint. This time she sucked it right down to her fingers.

"I prefer Bloody Marys," Diana said. "But in a pinch, V8 juice works." The gaze was working, too. The girl was locked in, swaying a bit, getting that dreamy look.

She handed back the roach, and Diana flicked it into the gutter.

"I don't have anything at my place," the girl said, "and it's halfway across town. I have a couple of bucks. We could stop at a store?" She paused, leaning closer, touched Diana's arm. Then: "Where do *you* live?"

They passed the bottle one more time, and Diana considered her options. The apartment was out—too much noise, too messy, and Darius —*DanielDanielDaniel!*—too much trouble. She knew the perfect spot, back in the park. She lit the second joint. This time the girl didn't shudder when she sipped, and she sipped again. She passed the bottle back, took the joint, and held Diana's touch for a couple of heartbeats.

Diana smiled and knew that between her gaze and that well-tested smile she had the girl in the whirl, right where she wanted.

"Let's go this way," Diana said, and linked arms with the girl. "I know a private spot with a bench. You'll love it."

Diana enjoyed a good fight more than seduction. She felt more complete, more whole, when they fought. Her life would be easier if her teeth were spikey, like in the movies, but then the fight wouldn't be quite as fair. Or quite as long. Her mother had preferred seduction and a well-placed nick with a well-honed, ivory-handled penknife, but Diana wanted the fight. It helped her to be more patient with her fastidious brother. Her own wounds would heal by sundown tomorrow.

Diana left her non-returnable Empty just before dawn in a small clearing protected by heavy brush. The sun would finish the rest, even in this perpetually gray climate. She was full and exhausted and ecstatic, so she nearly cut her shuffle home too close to the silver predawn sliver lightening the tops of the coastal range. She beat daylight and barely beat her brother who immediately wanted to load up and go, while she only wanted sleep.

CHAPTER FIVE

I n a second-floor bedroom of a Victorian house on the north coast of Washington, one figure stood zipping up pants next to the bed while another skootched upright against the pillows. The standing figure picked a uniform shirt off the back of a chair, "Sergeant Tom Aldrich" stitched over the right pocket, and slipped it on without buttoning. He lifted a corner of the window shade to see a quarter moon kissing the top of Marie's A Cut Above Hair Studio sign across the driveway. The courthouse clock on the next block bonged midnight. Tom bent down, kissed Marie Marceau, and buckled on his gun belt. He picked up his hat and shoes and kissed Marie again.

"Bye," he whispered. "I get off at ten this morning, but we're short-handed, so anything could come up."

"Bye," Marie whispered back. "If you're not working and still awake at noon, we could have lunch? Oh, except I'm already meeting Jean for lunch."

"Okay, I'll come by when I get off. We can make a plan then."

Marie reached up to ruffle Tom's hair. "While we're making a plan, let's make you an appointment. I know someone who's really good with hair."

Tom tiptoed the dark hallway past one bedroom door, his gun belt leather squeaking like an old saddle. A second bedroom door snapped open and a shadow swung at him with a baseball bat. Tom jumped aside, grabbed the wrist with the bat, shoved it behind the shadow's back,

19

snatched away the bat, and shoved the figure to the floor. The hallway light flashed on to reveal Tom with a knee in the middle of Marie's son's back.

"Stop!" Marie shouted. "What's going on here? James, are you all right?"

Tom stood and pulled James to his feet by the back of his t-shirt.

"I'm all right," Tom said. "Thanks for asking. Yes, James, what's going on here?" He tossed the bat back into James's room.

James tried to shake off Tom's grip, but Tom held him still.

"I thought you were a burglar," James said. His voice quavered and cracked. "I thought you were hurting my mom."

Tom shook his head and let the boy loose. Marie and her daughter, Lucy, looked on in shock.

"You could've dialed 9-1-1," Tom said. "Your mom got you that nifty phone."

A very pale James stood up straight and said, "Except 9-1-1 was busy sneaking around my house—"

"That's enough, James!" Marie snapped. "You kids, back to bed! We'll talk later. Tom has to work, and I have a full schedule tomorrow."

James stood and glared at Tom. Lucy looked between Tom, his shoes and hat on the floor, and her mom, wrapped in a sheet in the bedroom doorway.

"Mom!" she said. "You and Sergeant Tom?"

"Okay, enough!" Marie said. "Both of you, back to bed!"

Tom picked up his shoes and hat. Both kids slammed their doors. Marie turned up her hands in exasperation, and Tom smiled.

"Busted."

Marie tried not to laugh and waved him away with, "Oh, go catch a criminal."

CHAPTER SIX

D aniel unpacked the two units from the bottom of his cooler and cringed as he crammed them into the new extra-large incontinence underwear he'd lifted from the abdominal pain's bedstand. He settled them low in his crotch and breathed deep a couple of times to shake off the dick-shrinking chill. He pushed his supply cart back to lab stores and restocked before his lunch break.

His supervisor asked, "You're off tomorrow, right? Any chance you can come in for time-and-a-half?"

Daniel shook his head and tried to look sorry. "Taking my sister to an allergy specialist over in Boise," he said. "A promising clinical trial, and my sister likes her."

The supervisor shook his head. "We have some great people here in town. Why doesn't she want to—"

"She has severe social anxiety besides her allergies," he interrupted. "She likes this woman, so we're going to Boise."

His supervisor *humphed* and shook his head, tight-lipped. Daniel took his coat and briefcase from his locker and started for the exit. His supervisor stopped him with a hand on his shoulder. Daniel could smell the life of him, even taste it, so very close to his nose and mouth.

"Mr. Hunter," he said. "Why do you bring your lunch in that briefcase? Most people make do with a paper bag."

"I like my briefcase. Makes me feel professional."

"May I have a look?"

Daniel knew this was coming, knew that the other phlebotomist suspected something, but he'd come prepared. He raised his eyebrows, pressed his lips together, and stood straighter to look incensed. He handed over the briefcase.

"It's a nice one," his supervisor said. "What kind of leather?" He thumbed the latches and opened the case.

"Ostrich," Daniel said. "Been in the family for a couple of generations."

One uneaten sandwich, one baggie with crumbs.

"You didn't finish your lunch," he said.

"What's it to you? You my mother now?"

"Jesus, Hunter, stow the attitude!" His supervisor handed back the briefcase. "May I check your pockets?"

"What for?"

"Anything from the lab. Some inventory's missing and only since you got here. Inquiring minds want to know."

Daniel shook his head. "I'm no junkie!" he snapped. "Everybody knows the new guy'll always get blamed. Check the fucking coat and start advertising for a new phlebotomist." He tossed the coat at his supervisor's face, then took off his lab coat and threw that, too.

The startled supervisor caught the coats and took a couple of steps back.

"Don't get pissed at me," he said. "This is part of my job."

"Then get on with it," Daniel said. "I'm hungry and you're stealing my break time."

More indignation means more distraction.

Searching the two inner and two outer pockets of the overcoat and the two pockets of the lab coat took less than a minute and produced one opened travel-size pack of facial tissue, not from the hospital, and one rubber tourniquet for blood draws and IV starts. The supervisor dangled the tourniquet in front of Daniel's face. "Need this at home, Hunter?"

"I always keep an extra in my lab coat because nurses snatch them off my cart when they're in a hurry. It's efficient. Missing somebody's morphine?"

"Well ... no. Several units of whole blood."

Daniel snorted his impatience and said, "For what? My curbside transfusion service?"

The supervisor tossed back the coats and tried to stammer himself out of the situation.

"Look … I *know* your work's good … I mean … look, don't get so riled up. You're ruled out now and we can—"

"Let me go home?" Daniel interrupted. He unclipped his ID from the lab coat and dropped the coat to the floor, then shouldered his overcoat, pocketed his ID, and picked up his briefcase.

"Are you quitting?"

"If I'm not back for my next scheduled shift, mail my check." Over his shoulder, Daniel tossed, "HR has the address."

"Hey, now! Wait a minute!"

But Daniel didn't wait. He hurried to the parking lot, trying for an indignant but cautious stride. Already the IV bags chafed his freezing crotch. He gave his Uber driver an address several blocks from his storage unit and started rehearsing his argument for Diana.

An unfiltered unit should calm her down, he thought. *At least enough to get us out of town tonight.*

Daniel unlocked the storage warehouse and found their unmarked box truck just as the dead Proxy had promised and his sister had left it, their Mercedes wagon hitched behind on a trailer. The dead Proxy's new Lincoln was now in the hands of Darkest Knight, and Daniel regretted having to dump it. He had no gripe with equipment. His tools and lab gear appeared undamaged. Copper mesh panels from his clean room in San Francisco lined the walls, ceiling, and floor of the truck. Their emergency bed was set up, and the blackout curtain rolled up above the roll-up door. Cartons of his special sculpting clay were stacked against the cab wall, and he would need it immediately upon arrival in Salish Landing. He kicked the freezer holding the Empty and cursed his sister. New Washington plates front and back on both vehicles. New Washington ID for both of them on the truck's front seat. He found their cooler, placed the two units inside, and plugged it into the cigarette lighter.

He checked his watch, the map on his phone, the drive times on the map.

"Shit!"

Good thing he had an excuse to cut out so early in his shift. Still, he worried that they might not make it up the coastal highway by daybreak. He'd have to take the freeway and a ferry to make it in time, or they'd sleep in a rest area, always risky. He started the truck, saw that both tanks were full.

Good, no stops for gas. She'd better be ready to move.

Daniel found Diana insensible and snoring on the couch, her bloody hunting suit ripped around her chest and arms, scratches healing on her face and hands.

"Shit!"

He peeled off her soiled black silk and covered her in her least favorite caftan and bulky winter coat, then cut her bloody clothes into strips and flushed them down the toilet one by one.

No sign of blood anywhere else, he thought, with some relief. *She must've done this one outside.*

He packed his appliance, his tin of Matrix, their boxes and bug-out bags in the truck, then wrestled Diana upright and into the passenger seat.

"We go now?" Diana whispered. "You remembered Robert?"

She loved that plant, a gift from their mother long ago. Daniel had made a sun box for it, to fit between their blackout shades and the window.

Pain-in-the-ass plant that even needs special water.

She'd already slumped against her door, in a stupor or deep asleep. He raced back up to the apartment and retrieved her plant with all of its spiky, reddened leaves locked shut on drying blood. Daniel drove at the top of the speed limit along a seemingly endless corridor of trees and made the last ferry at 2:30 AM.

Daniel sipped a cold coffee and stretched his legs at the rail, surprised at how much marine traffic cruised through the night. Diana snored the whole way, which was just as well. He didn't have the patience to hear her latest story. The ferry's horn startled him and his cup dropped overboard. He never liked being on the water.

"Land-based life form," he muttered.

The ferry loudspeaker announced, "Welcome to Salish Landing. This is the last run of the night. All passengers must disembark."

Daniel pulled his overcoat collar closer and took in the few other cars as engines started up. He checked the hitch on the car trailer, climbed into the cab, started the truck and followed the ferry worker's signal down the ramp.

His dashboard clock read "3:45 AM." He drove down the nearly-deserted main street of Salish Landing, stopped under a streetlight and glanced at the sky.

"Close," he told no one.

He switched on the dome light and activated the map on his phone. He traced a highlighted yellow line with his finger from his downtown location along a winding road to a red mark on a bluff just out of town. A *tap-tap-tap* at his window startled him.

A police officer with the name tag "Sergeant Tom Aldrich" stood on the running board and gestured to roll down his window.

Aldrich flicked a glance at a sleeping Diana and smiled.

"Can I help you find someplace?"

Daniel manufactured a matching smile. Aldrich smelled full and warm. He'd also had sex recently. Daniel shifted his hunger to the cooler, swallowed hard and showed Aldrich the map.

"My sister and I bought this property at the end of Bluff Street. I think I've turned the wrong way."

"Bluff Street, huh?" Tom said. "That's the old Mandell place. They disappeared on a trip to California about a year back. Crazy about fishing."

"I didn't hear about that," Daniel said. "The county put it up for auction, and we got the lucky bid. The photos looked like a good deal, and I don't mind some work." His restless fingers played an imaginary tune on the steering wheel.

Tom nodded at Diana. "She's sure a sound sleeper! Well, congratulations, you won some of the nicest property in the county. House is finished, utilities in, but the garage—"

Daniel interrupted. "I'm sorry, officer, but we're really tired. Could you direct me …?"

Tom stepped down from the running board and touched the bill of his hat. "Of course," he said, "sorry. You don't have to turn around. Go left at that light up ahead, follow that road 4.2 miles to Bluff Road. You're at the very end, another half mile." He offered his hand and said, "I'm Tom, stuck on the night shift. Looking at two days off."

Daniel hesitated, then shook Tom's hand. "I'm Daniel …" he hesitated for a moment, searching for his new name. "Daniel Cazador." He nodded toward Diana. "My sister Diana there. We'll need a day or two off, too, before digging in to the house project. Thanks for the help."

His headlights illuminated the narrow, wooded drive and, finally, a large two-story house with an attached garage still under construction. Daniel pulled into the unfinished garage and hurried to the back of the truck, hands trembling. He flung open the roll-up door and his blackout curtain dropped on his face. He pinned the drape aside with a Velcro strap and hurried to Diana's door. Sweat pinned his shirt to his back; his breath came fast. He wrapped Diana's scarf around her face, picked her up and carried her to the back where he placed her on the bed. He reached to drop the roll-up door, yanked the blackout drape loose and flopped down exhausted next to Diana. His stomach cramped hard, but he'd left the cooler in the cab. No time to get to stasis. A nap would have to do. *Long day ahead.* He keyed his secure line with trembling hands and started the necessary calls.

CHAPTER SEVEN

Tom Aldrich leaned on the hood of his patrol car and watched a bright red dawn crawl its way over the Cascades to spill a blood-like sheen over the bay.

Red sky at morning, sailor take warning, he thought.

Two sailboats in the bay shifted at anchor to accommodate the morning breeze. His radio squawked.

A yellow sportfishing boat with *Fishkiller* on the side roared from the boat haven toward the mouth of the bay. Three bundled-up figures huddled in the cockpit and one waved toward Tom. Tom gave his brother the finger, shook his head, and opened his car door.

"Lucky bastards," he said to no one.

"Sixteen?" the radio said.

Tom keyed his mike. "Sixteen."

"Sheriff requests your assistance with traffic at the hot-rod shindig at the fairgrounds. Check-in starts in twenty minutes."

He watched his brother cut the power at mid-channel. All three figures scrambled to get lines in the water. Tom sighed.

"Roger, on my way."

Dispatch continued, "Tom, you-know-who called. She has a color demo going until at least ten tonight. Says come in quiet if you're coming over."

"Roger," Tom said. "And hello to everybody out there in scannerland."

Dispatch laughed and clicked twice.

Tom clicked back and did a quick drum roll on his steering wheel. He tossed his hat onto the passenger seat and headed for the fairgrounds. He passed the new skate park where Marie's son James practiced rails with his backpack on.

The kid's pretty good, he thought. *Glad he's at the park. I'd have to ticket him in the street.* He tapped the horn and waved, but James didn't look up.

Tom and his brother were raised by a single mom, and he remembered his resentment when she first started dating. He'd bulldozed one of her dates through the screen door and off the front porch when the man didn't take Tom's mother's "No" for an answer. He'd promised himself to be patient with Marie's kids. Lucy seemed to like him, but James was set on being a hard-ass. The kid would probably grow out of it, but the baseball bat incident indicated that it wouldn't be any time soon.

CHAPTER EIGHT

The sun was almost done with Mt. Olympus to the west, and James was late getting home to his chores after another round at the skateboard park. He started Weed Eating around his mom's A Cut Above Hair Studio sign without going inside first. He didn't want to face his mom after that incident with Tom and the bat. For the last two days, his anxiety had kept bringing up TV news reports about people shot by startled cops who thought they saw a weapon. Tom came by last night but didn't stay, and James kept to his room. He had skated hard for two hours after class to calm down today and worked up a sweat. Shirtless in the breezy afternoon air, he half-danced with the Weed Eater and listened to his buddy Dominic's new electronic music.

A car honked behind him in the driveway and startled him. He thought it was Tom and spun around to give him the finger, which did not look like a weapon. Jean, his mom's friend, waved from her ratty old Chevy. He was glad he'd held back the finger. The car had salt-air rust spots all over the bleached-out paint job so she called it "Pinto" even though it wasn't a Ford. Or that old. Her tilted magnetic sign on the door read "Jean's Sailboat Repair." He didn't see how anybody would hire her after seeing her car, but she was nice and good-looking for her age, which like his mom's was thirty-nine. His mom was happy when Jean stopped by. Today, he wanted his mom happy, and Jean stepped out of the car with a bottle of champagne.

"Hi, James," she said. "Is Marie finished for today?" Jean smelled like paint, as usual. Her bare arms had goose bumps from the chill and he tried not to look at her breasts, also goose bumping against her paint-spattered shirt.

James shut off the Weed Eater and lifted one earpiece.

"Yeah, probably," he said, and waved a hand toward the driveway. "No cars. She's probably sweeping up."

Jean ruffled his hair, which he never liked, on her way into the studio. At least she didn't pinch his cheek like some of his mom's clients. James fired up the Weed Eater and replaced his earpiece just as Tom pulled up in his patrol car. He pretended he didn't see or hear the car.

Tom rolled down his window and said, "James. Hey, James!" He rolled his eyes and hauled himself out of the car to tap James on the shoulder.

James turned but didn't lift his earpiece or shut off the Weed Eater. Or meet his gaze. Tom lifted an earpiece for him and smiled.

"Very nice job, James."

James leaned on the Weed Eater, crossed his arms, and stared past Tom at nothing.

Tom said, "I suppose it wouldn't do me any good to leave a message for your mom."

James said nothing and didn't look up. Tom erased his smile and sighed.

"Well, I had to work overtime again, and I need a nap. If you're in the mood, please tell Marie I'll be awake by ten if she wants company."

He carefully replaced James's earpiece and saluted "Goodbye." When Tom opened his car door, James said, "I guess those skateboard kids gave you a run down the Meridian hill this morning? Not as much fun at the park by myself. Why don't you chase down criminals instead of kids with no place to go?"

James's back was to Tom, and his headphones were full volume so Tom could hear the beat. He silently mimicked James behind his back, mouthing, *Why don't you chase down criminals instead of kids with no place to go?* Then he caught himself, laughed, shook his head, and said, "Gotta love 'em!" James didn't hear through the noise and the music.

Tom's home was a cold studio apartment in the top floor of another Victorian a few blocks from Marie's place. As usual, it was cold as death, even though news announced the first day of spring. He slipped around the foot of his pulled-out pull out bed and treated himself to a beer from his mini fridge. The only sound in the place was the hum of that fridge, and the only other living thing was a gangly ruby begonia beside the window. His sister had decided that he needed another living thing but didn't trust him with one of her dog's puppies.

"Caring for something else helps you care for yourself," she said. She'd studied psychology in college and wrote papers about their childhood. "Your girlfriend has kids. You need to learn to live with others."

He'd never married and blamed it on the job.

"I care for people," he'd countered. "That's my *job*!"

"There are different kinds of caring," she'd said. "Love, for example. That's Big Caring. Try it."

He kicked his rumpled covers aside and stretched out on his lumpy bed. The refrigerator shut off. He kicked off his shoes and listened to the silence. He used to like it. That was before Marie, and her kids, and their busy, happy household.

Maybe I should get K-9 training, he thought. He fell asleep dreaming about life with a dog as a partner, in the car and at home. It felt good. He'd need a bigger place. During his dream-debate of German Shepherd over Black Lab, he heard the faint *beep beep beep* of his phone from somewhere in the tangle of covers.

Sheriff's office. Fuck!

Both agencies were shorthanded, which meant the remaining personnel in each had to back up the other.

Tom cleared his throat and growled, "What now?"

"Jesus, Aldrich!" the Sheriff said, "Stuff the attitude. A couple having a romantic beach walk spotted an SUV nose down in the kelp bed at the end of Seven Dips Road. Couldn't see whether anybody's aboard. Wrecker's on the way. Do the on-scene report and I'll buy you dinner at 3 Crabs."

Tom tried rubbing the tired out of his face with no luck.

"Why don't you do it? You don't sound busy." Then Tom heard yelling in the background and the Sheriff taking a long drag from his cigarette. A loud crash.

"Mrs. Wilco is getting even with Mr. Wilco for coming home late," the Sheriff said. "And I know where he was, so I'm letting her blow off steam as long as she's busting up *things* and not *him* or our new first-grade teacher. Mrs. Wilco's a big girl who could clean his clock."

"Do you know how many dinners you already owe me?"

The Sheriff covered the phone to yell something at the Wilcos, then said, "Five. Are you helping or not?"

Tom sighed, stood up and stretched. "Okay, okay. Just save the dinner money and hire somebody for Chrissake!" He hung up, pulled on his rumpled uniform and headed back out into a darkening sky and half-hearted drizzle.

CHAPTER NINE

O n his first night in their new home, after being rested and fed, Daniel set up his office, complete with secured Wi-Fi hub, copper shielding, and computer array. Daniel contacted Darkest Knight to get a step ahead on protections, electronic and otherwise, that suited their situation. The scrambler would keep the sniffers on secret cellphone towers and nearby military bases at arm's length. The freezer with Diana's Empty inside sat under several shipping crates and a tarp in the unfinished garage. He found "Bill the Odd-Jobs Man" on Handyman.com and sent photos of their plans for the garage. Odd-Jobs Bill had a photo of himself and of several jobs that featured fine finish work. Daniel didn't need Bill for finish work—just to skin the unfinished exterior of the shop. Bill's photo, an off-center selfie, revealed long, graying hair that framed a tanned, mid-thirties face. His email address was the public library.

Daniel contacted the PODs people and their furnishings arrived over the next two nights, which stimulated a nesting gene in Diana and suspended the sullen gene she'd been packing for months. Three nights later he helped haul her personal gym upstairs to her office. Her level of exercise would spike her appetite. He needed to boost their backup supply pronto.

Half of the garage space would be Daniel's art studio. His tools and lab equipment hunkered in a pyramid of crates under tarps. His greatest worry came with the dangerous proximity of Diana to the various laborers assisting their move. She maintained by seriously depleting his refrigerated Matrix. He'd had to take a block out of the freezer this evening, way ahead of schedule.

The frozen should last a month, he thought, and shook his head. *At this rate, we'll be dry in two weeks.*

Odd-Jobs Bill replied from the library's computer with a bid within an hour. The bid was low, he could start immediately, and Daniel's need for speed boosted concerns about quality. Odd-Jobs Bill had 4.5 stars on Handyman. Comments about his work were glowing except one: "The guy's creepy quiet. Nothing missing, though." Daniel didn't mind "creepy quiet," so he copied down a list of materials, got the number for America's Lumber Supplies, and put in the order for tomorrow, including Diana's order for paint. He explained that they couldn't be reached during the day, sent Odd-Jobs Bill an advance through Venmo, and received a call-back immediately.

"We sleep during the day, so call or text," Daniel said. "One of us will answer."

"Gotta make noise," Bill said, "saws and all. What about that?"

Noise wouldn't bother them, but Daniel thought a moment. "Then finish up as soon as possible," he said. "You said four days?"

"Yes, sir. Good photos. Four days. That's pushing it."

"Push harder, make it two, and I'll double your bid."

Bill was quiet.

"Hello?" Daniel said. "You there?"

Bill cleared his throat and spit into something. "Can do," he said, "but I'll have to work evenings, too. Or hire some help."

Daniel didn't like the idea of more people around after dark. All his salon work would be after dark. So far, he'd only secured one place, and that was a demo. He had needs greater than money. He didn't want to decide between those needs and monitoring his sister, though her renewed fitness program and passion for design should keep her busy for a few days.

"My sister is a very private person," he said. "Let's keep it to you unless there's an emergency."

After that call, he created a Washington State LLC online for $75, opened a local bank account, and checked the secure server for messages from his Proxy. He received the address for a storage garage in Port Angeles, the passcode for the electronic gate, and the number of the garage.

He wanted to refit and restock their box truck and get it stored ASAP. The Proxy promised new ID, addresses of new rentals in both Canada and the US, and new contact info for him (or her) inside the cab within twelve hours. Daniel felt uneasy about the one-hour drive from Salish Landing to Port Angeles, but no local ferries sailed into Canada.

Daniel checked his phone for a map and was disappointed in the winding drive to Port Angeles but relieved that the truck storage was less than a block from the Canada ferry. He would have to pull everything out of the truck and rethink for emergency entry into Canada. Diana was restless already, and he worried about leaving the handyman alone with her. Daniel could be with Diana tomorrow, but that night was his first salon appointment, and Odd-Jobs Bill would be out there alone. After dark.

"I'll deliver the truck tonight," he told Diana. "I have my first appointment tomorrow. I'll have something for us when I get back. It's hard to find someone to do construction at night, so calm yourself. It's a small town. People miss people."

Diana smiled the kind of smile that fooled other people and said, "Look at you, the youngest, barking orders."

"Consider it a request. It's for our own good."

She kept the smile. "Say 'Please.'"

He knew that eye-rolling, exasperated sighs, physical signs of irritation would only make things worse, drag on longer.

"Please," he said, palms up in supplication. "Really, please."

"Okay, Brother," she said, "but you'd better deliver tomorrow. I can't wait much longer."

You mean you WON'T wait much longer, he thought, and hoped it didn't show.

"Remember," she said, without the smile, "this move was your fault for being careless. Twice before that we moved because of your *women*. *Please* control yourself." She raised her fingers for air quotes: "'It's for your own good.'"

"Mocking me doesn't help."

She picked up their new blue drapes and turned to the picture windows across the north wall.

"Maybe it doesn't help *you*, Brother, but *I* feel better."

He unpacked his new appliance, set it up in the dining room, then left in the truck for Port Angeles. This time he didn't leave his cedar puzzle-box in the truck with IDs and credit cards. Considering that one-hour drive, he wanted some security if he had to flee without the truck.

She's too erratic, he thought. *If she unravels, and I have to run ...*

Daniel pushed the thought aside and focused on his mission. He met the only Uber in Port Angeles at the ferry landing and pretended he'd just crossed from Canada. He wanted a garrulous driver, brimming with local lore and opinions about local salons, health clubs, and spas. Instead, his driver switched the car to autopilot and spent his time reading Sartre's *No Exit.* Daniel didn't collect any local lore, but he did feel ignored, therefore invisible, which was the next best thing. He got out at Four Corners Store anyway and walked the last mile to their house, grateful that the rain had let up. First on his mind was his inaugural product demo tomorrow evening at A Cut Above Hair Studio.

Owner had a nice phone voice, he thought. *Good sign.*

CHAPTER TEN

Marie flipped up the shade and a rosy-fingered dawn topped the Cascades, smearing a palm of pink between blue sky and a few puffy clouds. She flopped back onto her bed and touched her sweaty forehead to Tom's. After a sixteen-hour shift, he'd been exhausted when he slipped off his shoes inside Marie's back door and stocking-footed his way to her room. He pulled her closer and said, "What got into you tonight?"

She laughed. "Why, *you*, you silly man. It must be the uniform."

"But I'm naked."

She sighed and kissed him, then looked him up and down. "Exactly."

Tom rolled to the side of the bed to get to the bathroom, and Marie swung her hand around to tug his pubic hair.

"Oh no you don't," she said. "The kids already busted you sneaking out, so you might as well stay."

Her hand slid farther. Tom rolled back. "What, and face the … the *kids*?"

He mimed wide-eyed terror and pulled the covers up to his face. He didn't have much experience with kids long-term, close-range. He made conversation, and he could tell that the kids could tell he was trying.

Marie's hand found its target under the sheets. She snuggled closer and whispered, "The kids know. The school knows. Pretty much everybody in town knows. When did *you* know, Tom?"

He liked what her hand was up to, but his bladder already had all the pressure it could take. The bathroom was halfway down the hall, right across from James's room.

"I really need the bathroom," Tom said. "Really. Do you have an extra robe or something?"

"Just mine," she said. "It'll be a little short on you, but you'll look cute, all pink and everything." She plucked her robe from the bedpost and tossed it to him.

"Oh, Geez!" He wrapped it around himself and it came nearly up to his butt. "Oh, Geez!"

"Better hurry," she said. "Or there'll be a line."

Fortunately, the kid coming out of the bathroom was Lucy, who said, "Good morning, Tom," and skipped to her room with a giggle. He hoped James wouldn't be there when he came out. The town skaters would never let him live down that frilly, pink mini-robe.

CHAPTER ELEVEN

Daniel couldn't sleep after his slip with the Uber driver. He'd been tired and entered one of his old names, "Darrel," to make the reservation. Unfortunately, he used the new "Cazador," not "Darrel Cacciato" from three years ago, or his recently abandoned "Hunter."

I was tired and hungry, he thought. *Diana's right. I'm getting careless.*

"Tighten the fuck up!" he told himself, and got busy.

He ordered new, insulated blackout shades with Velcro trim for all the windows, expedited one-day delivery. Even one leak through their new drapes was too much for Diana, and when Diana was uncomfortable, everyone was uncomfortable. He didn't trust Diana with people in the house. Already he worried about Bill the Odd-Jobs Man working in the garage. She was attractive, deliberately sultry when on the hunt, happy with women or satisfied with men in a pinch. Men were easier in the short term. Diana managed their interior world while Daniel focused on the exterior. Hanging blackout shades and painting the interior were her immediate tasks after their PODs delivery, their good furniture and her workout equipment.

Much as she hates to move, he thought, *she loves making a place her own.*

Problems came when paint dried, pictures were hung, furniture set in its places, and boredom hardened her like concrete. He'd tried to sell her on his Matrix by asking, "Did you ever find a woman you'd like to stay with for a long time? This could help that."

She twisted up a disgusted face and shook her head.

"I can't afford one of your 'relationships,'" she said. "Things go wrong out there in the light. People who like you want you to meet people *they* like, who want to inspect you, judge you. They have *families*." She shuddered, and her gaze hardened on the past. She almost told him about the impossible pregnancy, then waved a hand in dismissal. "Besides, you're talking about cattle. Milk them a little twice a day? Or nick them in the neck with Mother's little ivory-handled pocket knife like she did in her made-up religious schtick?" She shrugged and studied the unpainted wall behind him. "They're not worth the trouble. I won't die like Mother!"

Daniel's computer held a scan of the newspaper account of the discovery of their mother's remains. DNA hadn't been discovered yet when she died, but officials found her handbag and her special collection kit with a small glass container of blood, type O negative. New Mexico state police described her remains as "… a charred smear of baked bone fragments, a few teeth and black goo alongside Portrero Ditch outside Chimayo. Looks like she'd been dumped and set afire alive. She almost made it to the water."

Diana's response at the time was a vacant stare and a shrug. "She messed with the Gypsies."

"Manner of death: 'Suspicious.'"

"Possible causes of death: 'Satanic Ritual' (being Holy Week), 'Personal Vendetta' (two client/patients disappeared), 'Spontaneous Human Combustion' (no residue of combustibles present)."

She burned to death in the sun on the morning of Good Friday, so all manner of Christians became suspect.

"You really think it was the Gypsies?" he'd asked.

Same vacant stare, deadpan; she said, "They came through every year. She came to town and took away business. Lured her late at night, maybe a new client. Kicked her out before dawn to walk back. Didn't know about our … allergy. End of Mother." She cracked a smile.

"What's so funny?"

She shook her head. "Irony, Brother. Try to keep up."

Daniel gave up on sleep and flipped on his bedroom light, a strip of red LEDs, easiest on his eyes. His workshop wasn't ready, so he rolled the remaining tin of his Matrix out of his mini fridge to a marble-topped maple dresser he'd made two moves ago. He set out a carton of squeeze bottles stamped with "Mr. Daniel's Miracle Matrix." He would've used

"Dr." as he did with his other, less successful inventions, but the famous corporate cosmetologists liked to be "Mr." He printed out a new set of business cards as "Mr. Daniel, BioCosmetologist." He'd studied biochemistry in a half-dozen night schools and found none that offered complete night programs. He supplemented with some of the best science libraries, but he needed the night schools for the labs. His night-school colleagues made excellent experimental subjects. The few who got suspicious got blind dates with Diana.

She was "Deirdre" then, after our Mother.

Deirdre was the only name his twin used more than once, a security breach that troubled him but boosted the thrill for Diana.

Daniel studied years of engineering on top of the biochemistry to tinker up his exfusion appliance. He still couldn't infuse the Matrix with the correct dose of the fresh, raw adrenaline to satisfy Diana's palate. Epinephrine from the hospital squirted into the mix made it bitter and made her manic for two days. He hadn't managed to fine-tune exfusion —still an all-or-nothing filter. Diana didn't miss the bitter edge of testosterone, which, for her, was easier to get.

She says bland is the problem, he thought, *but she gets off on the hunt. The hunt is one whole-body fuck for her.*

Daniel preferred actual sex with actual women, along with a good Bordeaux and, if they had it, weed. He couldn't risk having a taillight out, much less a bag of weed in the glove box, even if it was legal. He avoided driving around at all, which was easier in cities. Already out here the edge of the earth looked like trouble.

That cop homed in on us right away.

He stuffed each squeeze applicator with a half-pound of Matrix, then placed the tin and a baker's dozen of full bottles into his fridge. Preparation always made him eager. To calm his trembling hands, Daniel practiced slow, deep breaths to lead him into stasis. He lay down to pass the day before his first professional appearance at A Cut Above.

CHAPTER TWELVE

Daniel parked his Mercedes wagon in the hair salon's driveway beside two cars and a bicycle. He approached the lighted shop window and over the crunch-crunch of gravel heard women laughing and the clink of glassware. Two women drank champagne through long glass straws and made that sucking sound when they reached the bottom. One woman with the champagne poured all three of them another round.

The woman pouring must be Marie of the nice voice, he thought. She looked nice, too, in a northwest-country-plaid sort of way.

A tall, slender, dark-haired woman with native features wore overalls and a "Plant Native" t-shirt. He noted her athletic build and supposed she owned the bicycle out front.

Diana would like her, he thought. *She needs somebody to like besides her flytrap.*

The other woman looked about forty, with strawberry blonde hair like Diana's and freckles spattered across patches of sunburn. Her tight yellow "Jean's Sailboat Repair" t-shirt and red yoga pants revealed narrow dancer's hips and long, very fit legs.

Only three, he thought. *Really, only two!* He masked his disappointment with a smile.

Daniel had hoped for at least six people, a stable and a pantry, of sorts. Neither he nor Diana could afford disappointment, and the life he wished for hinged on the success of this venture. Marie waved him inside for introductions, flashed him a smile, made good eye contact and offered a firm, warm handshake.

"We're enjoying champagne, would you like some? Also we have coffee and little triangle sandwiches that Alice brought."

Daniel smelled hot blood blushing up the Plant Native's deeply tan neck and face.

Tan? He wondered. *Ethnicity?* Northwest people were hard to peg among the mix of Asian Americans, Pacific Islanders, Native Americans, and caravans of gypsies who rolled up from California every year after Easter.

She dropped her gaze and acknowledged with a quick, waist-high wave. He imitated her wave back, and she cracked a smile but still didn't meet eye to eye.

Daniel turned to the tray of sandwiches, generated a look of interest eclipsed by regret. "They smell delicious," he said. "A smoked meat of some kind?"

Alice glanced at Jean, then Marie, who nodded in support, then the sandwiches.

"Smoked elk," Alice said.

A quiet, clear voice.

Alice cleared her throat and spoke a little louder, "My Dad. East of the mountains."

"A rare treat!" he said. "I'll try one while you three are relaxing."

Daniel unpacked his sample case and set three of his squeeze bottles onto the countertop. He shook hands with Alice of the sandwiches and overalls, and with Jean of the freckled sunburn. He envied a sunburn that wouldn't kill him.

He explained the exfusion process and told them what to expect.

"It gets warm, tingles, turns from gray to pink," he said. "While removing toxins, it tightens the skin and erases wrinkles. A light exfoliation also occurs, so please wash your faces clean of other products before we proceed."

Marie handed out hot towels from a hamper beside their chairs, and they took turns at the shampoo sink. Marie tossed the used towels into another hamper and sat first. Daniel gently massaged the gray goo onto her face. She closed her eyes and enjoyed the massage with a smile.

"It's getting pretty warm?" she said, in the American way of asking a statement. "How hot does this get?"

"Warm is normal," he said. "It comes up to body temperature and pulls blood to the surface. Pulls the good things in, pushes the bad things out."

He massaged gray goo masks onto Alice and then Jean.

"Yours is changing already, Marie," Jean said. "It's as pink as my nose."

"Then it firms up with a tingle, gets red," Daniel said. "Then, no lines."

"Very nice tingle," Alice said. "What does this cost, usually?"

Daniel and Jean met each other's gaze. Parts of Jean not covered with goo flushed red. He smiled.

"Marie has an intro rate," Daniel said. "Rates would change depending on numbers and frequency."

Marie didn't answer right away, and he didn't elaborate. Money was not important to him, just the product. The only sounds were the heater hum, the scuff of Daniel's shoes on black-and-white checkerboard linoleum, the fizz of champagne as he filled their glasses. Marie finally answered in a dreamy, faraway voice.

"Depends on his success, he means," Marie said. "We get a break for helping with his startup. We need to spread the word so he sticks around."

"The price?" Alice stage-whispered.

Daniel positioned their glasses and straws so they could sip through their goo.

"Daniel gets fifty dollars for the hour, then ten per person for the mix."

"So," Jean said, "for five people it's twenty bucks apiece." She spoke to Marie but kept her gaze on Daniel. The other women relaxed in their chairs, eyes closed. Nobody spoke.

Jean cleared her throat and said, "Such a deal!"

Marie roused herself and replied in a whisper, "That's my cost. I'd have to add ten apiece to make it worth my shop time. Plus a freebie for myself, of course. Thirty dollars to start."

Alice said, "This is bliss for thirty dollars. An earthquake couldn't move me now."

Daniel checked each mask and spoke softly to all. "Be sure to wait another hour before driving, especially after your champagne. You'll be too light in the head."

Jean tried to capture her straw and didn't see that she had a glob of red goo on the end. Her lips almost closed on it when Daniel plucked it away, startling Jean. He regained her gaze and showed her the glob of red.

"Not for the insides," he said, and winked. "Just for the outsides."

He turned to the sink, tapped the glob into his palm and stopped his tongue from licking it up. He rinsed the straw, turned back to the table and smoothly pressed the glob back into Jean's mask, holding her cheek for a couple of beats. He placed the straw into her drink and the other end at her lips. His fingers touched and lingered on her lips for just a moment. She gave them a tiny kiss and giggled.

"Thank God for light in the head," Jean said.

The other women giggled, then relaxed to the point of dozing. All masks darkened from pink to red. Daniel nibbled at a sandwich while he circled their chairs, tested the goo on each face with a finger. Smoked meats never agreed with him, but he choked it down with an appreciative smile.

"Interesting," he told Alice. "Never had elk."

Again, he lingered over Jean, unable to resist the lightest touch on her neck and shoulder. Jean smiled without opening her eyes.

"This is to die for," she said.

Marie leaned farther back in her chair while Daniel gently peeled the soggy, red mask from her face. Eyes still closed, she said, "I dreamed I was flying. Long, featherless wings. Just a slit of moon." She paused. "A little sting when you pulled it away."

Daniel formed the pack into a red mud-ball and slipped it into a large plastic bag. Alice and Jean looked fast asleep, so he watched them for a moment. Alice could be Diana's type, for sure. He'd have to be careful there. He still liked Marie's voice, but his real attraction was to Jean. The suddenness of it surprised him. He peeled off Alice's pack. Even her darker complexion had a glow.

"I feel kind of disoriented," Marie said.

Daniel worked Alice's pack into another ball and said, "That's normal. Your blood vessels expanded, your pressure is lower. Except for that champagne, no more toxins. Relax and enjoy."

Daniel added the second pack to his collection bag.

"Feels illegal," Alice whispered.

"BioCosmetology," Daniel said. "I started in biochemistry, and one thing led to another. I have a patent. Really, it was an engineering problem."

Alice smiled, eyes closed, and said, "Just kidding."

Daniel peeled away Jean's blood-red pack, placed it into the collection. Jean's eyes fluttered open.

"Marie," she said, "that's the best thirty dollars I ever spent."

Jean stood and reached for her drink. Vertigo spun her half-around and she grabbed the counter to get her bearings. Daniel caught her by the shoulders to guide her gently back to her chair.

"Please don't move yet. Just relax while I finish cleaning up."

Jean winked at Marie then leaned back in her chair, closed her eyes, breathed deep. Daniel removed steaming towels from Marie's warmer and wiped each woman's face clean. A rusty, reddish hue stained the towels that he tossed into Marie's linen basket. Jean opened her eyes that shone with a new glitter.

"Isn't this how heroin addicts start?" she asked. "A freebie?"

Daniel kept his hands on Jean's shoulders.

"I'm glad you enjoyed it," he said. "It's really un-addiction, the removal of addicting compounds from the blood."

Jean asked, "God, can we do this every day? Can I *afford* this every day?"

Daniel turned serious and put up a warning hand.

"No," he said. "Better for me financially to do more, but it's good for the face once a week. You don't want to work your beautiful skin too hard with anything."

"Pity," Marie said, "I'd make a fortune."

Jean laughed and said, "I know you. You'd go broke lying up in your room with your face pack on."

Daniel placed the collection bag into his black leather case.

Marie said, "You can throw those in my garbage, if you want."

Daniel felt his expression harden and immediately softened his gaze, smiled his best you-can-trust-me smile.

"I'm still refining the process," he said. "You described a little sting, so I'll analyze these and see how to work that out."

"Protecting your secrets?" Jean asked.

He thought, *You have no idea.*

As though she read his mind, Marie told Jean, "The product world is a cutthroat business. Pays to be careful." She handed mirrors to Alice and Jean. "You two, look at yourselves!"

Jean moved the mirror closer, farther, and gushed, "This was me *before* all the sun and salt water! Do I really have so many freckles?"

Alice stared at the mirror, ran her fingers across her forehead and down her cheeks. "I can't believe it," she whispered.

Marie patted Daniel's shoulder and asked, "When can we schedule you again?"

He checked his phone, feigned scrolling through a calendar.

"A week from today?" he asked. "I can't recommend any sooner."

Marie nodded, closed her eyes and sat back. "One whole week," she sighed. "Okay with you, ladies?"

"Yes!"

"Absolutely!"

He marked his calendar. "Okay, one week from today. Please, keep the group small, no more than six. Otherwise, it's an assembly line and not as much fun." Daniel and Jean exchanged smiles and maintained eye contact.

Jean said, "Maybe you need an assistant. And this goo needs a sexy name. I'll bet you patented under the unpronounceable chemical name."

"Well, yes …"

"See, you need a manager, too!"

"Just don't take his prices out of our range!" Marie said. "I'd better write that down in my book."

Marie started to get up but Daniel's gentle hand on her shoulder placed her back onto her chair. She marveled for a moment at the dream-like light that suffused the room.

"Relax," he said. "I'll write everything on my card."

He uncapped an old-fashioned fountain pen and wrote the details on the back of his card in beautiful calligraphy, including his new email address. The printed side read only "Mr. Daniel, BioCosmetology." He glanced at Jean, who winked, then added his cell phone number. He gave Jean a slight bow and said, "I'll see you in a week."

He washed his hands, picked up his case, and quietly let himself out.

Jean closed her eyes again and leaned back in her chair. "I can't let that one get away, Marie. If you don't give me his number, I'll strangle you in your sleep."

Alice, a little wobbly getting out of her chair, asked, "Where will you get the energy?"

"Tomorrow," Jean said. "I'll come by and strangle her tomorrow."

Alice steadied herself on the back of her chair and said, "He's the *whitest* guy I've ever seen! Maybe he bleaches."

"Whiter than Jean," Marie said. "But Jean has freckles to break up the glare." She stood slowly and offered Jean a hand up. "I have to get to the kids. You two be careful driving."

CHAPTER THIRTEEN

Diana waited half an hour after Daniel drove away before she opened the garage's utility door to watch Bill the Odd-Jobs Man nail up the last sheet of plywood on the garage exterior. She'd been good this time and painted her room glossy black and the living room a deep cobalt blue. He'd started on the garage at 8:00 AM. She'd asked him not to use his nail gun, so he hand-nailed for the rest of the day and into the evening, finally, using a headlamp. Working alone, he hadn't been able to finish the exterior by dark. She'd heard a lot of creative cursing as he manipulated each sheet of plywood alone. A stack of sheetrock awaited Daniel's work on the interior. The old blue pickup with "Bill the Odd-Jobs Man" on the doors stood next to one of Daniel's grotesque sculptures, almost human-looking, primitive, not quite covered under a tarp —their dead Proxy, an insurance adjustor in life. Diana's indiscretion. Other tarps covered Daniel's crates of tools, supplies and lab equipment stacked against the wall of the house. Nothing appeared disturbed.

Daniel should've shipped that piece already, Diana thought. *He's getting very careless.*

The calligraphy on the battered old truck intrigued her for its grace and beauty next to its owner, scruffy-haired in paint-spattered jeans but cleanly shaven. Daniel had noted immediately that the odd-jobs man had red hair and blue eyes: "The rarest genotype," he'd said. She liked red hair and deepened the color of hers often because it emphasized the effect of her green eyes. Bill worked without a shirt, his well-muscled arms and back shiny with sweat and a smattering of sawdust. The truck radio played blues from a Canadian station across the Strait. He drove the last nail with a "Hoo-rah!" then hit the switch to the garage door and did a little dance to Taj Majal playing "Squeeze Box." Bill stopped dancing and blushed when he saw Diana silhouetted in the light from the utility room. He reached inside the truck and shut off the radio.

"Sorry, Ms. Cazador, but it's been a long day."

She wore her painting overalls with their strategic straps that moved when she moved so he could see she was naked underneath.

She laughed to set him at ease.

"No worries," she said. "You've done the work of two men today, that's worth some celebration. Would you like a beer to go with your dance? And please call me Diana."

"Yes, Ms. ... Diana, I'd love a beer."

She flashed her best come-fuck-me smile. "Excellent!" she said. "Oh, could you bring that extra tarp in with you? The large one? I want to paint a fancy trim of leaves across the top of the living room wall."

"Got it," he said. He peeled off his headlamp, pulled on his Hawaiian shirt emblazoned with toucans that don't live in Hawaii, then yanked the tarp from the truck, hefted it onto his shoulder and followed her into the house.

He stepped into the doorway of the now blue-dark living room with its blackout shades and felt the wall for the light switch. Diana gripped his wrist to stop him.

"Oh, I prefer the dark, don't you?" She shifted her grip to holding his hand. "I like to watch the lights of Canada come on. Bring it over here."

She led him to the north end of the room, rolled up a blackout shade and slid apart a set of heavy blue drapes. The huge picture window overlooked the Strait and revealed a faint string of lights glimmering through an early wisp of fog. A window box with her satiny black flytrap stuck out from a panel beside the frame. Her plush blue couch faced the view instead of the living room.

"Here," she said, and patted the couch. "Tarp from the window, over the couch and over this stretch of carpet. I'll get your beer."

She returned with two beers, handed him one and set a second on the windowsill.

"Thanks," he said, and tilted his head. "'Bloody Beer'?" He held up the bottle to study the label: A bloody axe next to a bloody chopping block with pools and spatters of blood over the scene.

"A lager brewed with fermented tomato juice," she said. "Peppercorns and horseradish, too. My brother's favorite."

"Looks like the red beer old-timers used to drink around here. You'd drop a little can of tomato juice into your beer, like dropping in a jigger of whiskey for a boilermaker."

"Sounds dreadful," she said.

"Probably the only vegetable those old guys got." Bill toasted her with the bottle and slugged half of it down in one breath. "Holy cow!" he said and smacked his lips. "That's one hot drink." His eyes watered but he downed another slug. Bill remained at the window, studying Diana more than the view. She plopped onto the tarp-covered couch and patted the spot next to her. Her straps fell away perfectly. "Nice view, no?" she said. "Now, let's sit for a minute. Or do you have to get home to your family?"

Bill finished the rest of his beer in a long swallow, triggered a coughing fit, then set the empty on the windowsill. He sat at the other end of the couch.

"Naw, Diana, I live alone. Unless you count the mold on the cheese in my icebox."

Diana laughed. "You say 'icebox,'" she said. "You don't hear 'icebox' much these days. Always 'the fridge.'"

"That's because it's really an icebox," he said. "Old-fashioned, nickel-plated corners and handles. Have to feed it a block of ice a week is all. I'm off the grid."

She scooted closer. "Does that explain the moldy cheese?"

"Yeah." Bill swallowed hard. "Cheese does that." He cleared his throat. "Molds."

Diana stood to fetch his second beer and walked around to the back of the couch. She reached over his shoulder and placed the cold bottle right in his crotch. He snatched it up like it could bite. Diana combed his hair back over his ears with her fingers, whispered, "Why don't you stay here for a bite?"

"Well, I ..."

Diana grasped his hair and in one blur of movement yanked his head back and bit hard and fast into his neck with a wet, deep growl. His legs and arms flailed backwards in the near dark as she pulled him over the back of the couch. Bill screamed and his nails dug deep into her arms before she crunched his trachea with both hands. He fought hard for a minute, two, but she'd trained for this her whole life. Stronger and faster than he could've guessed, and ferocious. She chewed deeper and her tongue found his carotid. Hot blood spurted over her and the tarp.

What a waste!

Her techie brother still hadn't invented a single-handed way to save it. Now, again, she wished for fangs like their mother described their father's, like the movies. Diana'd never met him, but their mother had described him many times; always in the telling she looked rapturous as a teenager at a rock concert, which she had been.

A hairline groove down the backs of his special teeth injected an intoxicating anesthetic into his bite. Tiny serrations glistened at the edges like Clovis blades and fairly melted through flesh. Neither Diana nor her brother had met their father, nor any remaining of his kind.

Diana's crude, messy method sometimes dislocated her jaw or a shoulder in the struggle. This time, Bill's legs quivered then lay still as she gurgled and sucked herself breathless. She lay down beside him on the tarp for the satisfying, stupefying buzz. The testosterone undertones were hardly detectable at all.

CHAPTER FOURTEEN

The open, insulated satchel with the fully-charged Matrix sat on the passenger seat beside Daniel. He drove to Bach on the CD, his hand caressing the plastic bags inside. He closed the satchel, patted it, shook the tremble from his hands and returned to driving Bluff Road in the misty dark. Hunger slung him into a dangerous slide on the last curve of his tree-lined driveway. Daniel smiled when his headlights revealed the enclosed walls of the garage.

That's a lot of progress for one man in a day!

He hit the button on the garage door opener and timed his clearance precisely. His smile turned grim at the sight of Bill the Odd-Jobs Man's truck, the faulty tarp job on his most recent sculpture, the quiet house, and the absence of Bill. The door to the utility room opened to silhouette Diana holding her battered, bloody overalls up to her chest by its remaining strap.

"Brother Dear," she slurred, her voice languorous, "how was *your* hunting?"

She smiled with a Joker's smear of blood across her mouth, chin, neck ... *Everywhere!*

"You didn't ...!"

"Wait?" She lost her grip on the doorframe and nearly fell. "I waited. Then ... I quit waiting."

Daniel raised his satchel, slapped it three times and said, "I have three right here. No contamination, no danger of passing our infection, *no deaths!*"

He brushed past Diana, who leaned dreamy-eyed in the doorway.

"He's in the living room not living," she said. "Might as well stake him now."

"The carpenter?" he shouted.

She nodded, barely awake.

"Yes. Bill." Her voice was soft, tinged with a note of fondness. "The Odd-Jobs Man."

Diana followed Daniel to the kitchen where he lifted his three bags of red goo out of the case. He dampened his urge to look into the living room. His hands now trembled out of anger and hunger. He breathed deep to regain control.

Inhale: *This is not new.*

Exhale: *Ducks in a row.*

Inhale: *This is not new.*

She leaned against the refrigerator, her eyes nearly closed. "How long can you function on that?" she asked.

Daniel exhaled slowly and unbagged the first of his wages for the night.

"A month," he said. "Maybe more. A really wild week. I do like other food."

Diana snorted her derision and a light spray of blood hit the table. She wiped a finger across it and licked her finger. She steadied herself against a chair.

"*Their* food." She rolled her eyes and nodded at the bag. "That wouldn't get me through the night. And you still *need* our food."

Daniel pulled his appliance from the shelf and slopped a handful of goo into the top. He said, "Martini," placed a coffee cup under the spout and focused on the output. He was too angry to look at her.

"It's all learned," he said. "You could learn to live on less. I have."

"Blah-blah," she said. "Pitiful quantity. Bland bland bland."

The whirring of the machine stopped. He picked up the cup, looked inside and had to agree with her about "pitiful quantity." He sniffed the product then tossed it back. His trembling hands settled down immediately, but his anger remained.

"No toxins with bland," he said, "and no competition. You don't infect every carpenter and insurance agent ..."

She smiled. "He was an adjustor. He's adjusted himself into a nice sculpture in your shop."

Daniel took her by the arm and led her into their dark, vaulted living room. He walked her around Bill's drained body on the tarp and up to their picture window. Diana looked fondly at Bill's remains.

"Really," she said, and shook her head, "you should do something about the waste."

He ignored her and watched the skiff of fog lift enough to reveal the lights across the Strait. He was too angry to look at her.

"This is our first real home," he said, voice tight in his throat. "I've been years edging us into this place, covering traces, cleaning up. You've said you're tired of running? Then just *stop*. Look over there at the lights of Canada. Beautiful house, beautiful view ..."

"Like Mother used to say, 'Every light is a hot meal waiting.' Don't lecture me. Your women have caused plenty of trouble."

"That's sex," he said, "they move on. Humans call this murder. They move in."

Diana giggled and sat in her favorite leather recliner to enjoy the view—Canada across the water, and Bill asprawl the tarp.

"I'm the oldest, Brother Dear."

He turned to face her and watched her eyes droop on their way to stupor.

"Twelve minutes in two hundred years means nothing to me," he said.

Her head snapped to attention, her green eyes aglitter in the dark.

"It means I live as I want to live or die trying!"

Daniel waved a hand to indicate what used to be Bill. "You could stake them yourself, at least."

Diana waved back a lethargic dismissal. "But I don't care. And you do. I gave the last one to the sun. You stake him. I need a nap." She curled up in her chair and closed her eyes.

Daniel's cell phone chirped. He looked at Bill's body, at Diana. His phone chirped again.

Diana spoke, barely above a whisper, "Found another little toy, did you?"

The phone chirped again. Daniel said, "It's not like that. Not this time."

She was asleep already, her Joker smile imprinting on the leather chair.

Daniel swiped the screen with a trembling finger and said, "Hello, Daniel Cazador."

"Hi," Jean said, "it's Jean, from tonight. I hope you don't mind the call."

Daniel took the call to the kitchen and reloaded his appliance.

"I just poured a nice glass of white wine and wondered why I wasn't calling you, so I called. I hope it's all right?"

"Yes, of course," he said. "How nice to hear from you." He moved the phone aside, said, "Martini" and placed his cup. "I was just fixing a drink myself. Still relaxing?"

"Very relaxed … and not driving on alcohol, as you advised."

The line was quiet for a moment while he sipped at his second helping.

"I was going to ask Marie for your number tomorrow," he said.

Daniel heard the gurgle of wine into a glass. "You were?" Jean said. "Well, now I don't feel so foolish calling you. I'm not usually this forward."

Another sip and he folded into the conversation. "How forward are you? Usually?" He placed the remainder of the bag into his refrigerator.

"Well, not this forward," she said. "I work with a lot of people, mostly men. Mostly, I ignore them for my own good. I don't want to ignore you."

Daniel tossed back the last of his drink and sighed. He felt normal for the first time in days.

"Lucky for me," he said. "Do you have an evening free this week? I care for my sister during the day, so evenings are best." He licked the rim of his cup and set it aside.

"How about tonight?" Jean asked. "It's still early, and cozy here on the boat. C dock, slip five. Sailboat *Freedom*."

Daniel glanced back at the mess in the living room.

"I'm just finishing dinner, and I have a few things to clean up before I leave my sister."

"Take your time," Jean said. "I'm an insomniac, awake most of the night."

Daniel chuckled and said, "What a coincidence, so am I!"

CHAPTER FIFTEEN

Marie set down her phone and sipped the last of the champagne while James dished up strawberry rhubarb pie and ice cream for himself and Lucy. She felt not so much tipsy as dislocated or dissociated while the room around her glowed the way images glowed after photographers smeared Vaseline on their lenses.

Otherworldly, she thought. She liked it. Everything seemed ... *nice*.

"Jean called him and he's meeting her on the boat," she said. "They couldn't keep their eyes off each other."

"I thought you learned your lesson about that matchmaking stuff after you fixed Alice up with a man," James said. "He's a *stranger*. Give it a few weeks first."

Marie dropped the bottle into her recycling and sat back down, a little whirly.

"Look at you, all mature about relationships," she said. "This is different. You should have seen the two of them—*so* cute!"

James turned to Lucy and gestured a finger down his throat.

"Gag me!"

Lucy spoke through a mouthful of pie. "What do you know about anything?"

"I know you're not supposed to talk with your mouth full. I know I'm never going to be *cute*!"

"No lie, lizard," she said.

Marie waved a hand and said, "Cool it, you two. Why don't you take the laptop to James's room and pick out a movie?"

James thumped the table and rattled the dishes. "All right!" he said. *"Braveheart!"*

Lucy rolled her eyes. "Men in skirts with bare butts and big swords," she said. "I worry about you."

Marie stood slowly, one hand gripping the table for security. "Watch something quiet," Marie said. "I'm really tired. I'm going to bed."

James leaned closer to Marie and said, "Is *Tom* coming over?"

Marie put her hands on her hips, raised her eyebrows and sighed.

"What?" James said. "Do you know how tough things get at school when your mom's dating a cop?"

"We're not dating," she said. She smiled and stacked the dinner dishes in front of her. "You both were dreaming."

Lucy said, "Oh, brother. 'Dreaming.'"

"We'll be dreaming again tonight, I suppose," James said. "He said he's coming by after work."

"Ah," Marie said. "Well. I guess I won't be going to bed yet after all." She turned too fast and recaptured the edge of the table. "Whew! Too much champagne. I'll put on coffee and you two better get moving. Dishes, homework, movie, bed."

James picked up the stack of dishes and set them in the sink.

"Let's go! My turn to pick!"

"You picked last time!"

"American Werewolf in London," James said. "That was yours."

Lucy said, "Okay, okay. But vampire movies are quiet. How about *Bride of Dracula*?"

Marie interrupted. "Homework. Dishes. Movie. Bed. In that order, please."

Lucy picked up a necklace with an oversized silver cross and put it on. The cross hung nearly to her belly. James rolled his eyes and sighed the teenage sigh for adults who just can't keep up. "We did homework while you were demo-ing."

Marie shuffled to the sink and stared at the dishes. They swept in and out of focus. Colors that didn't have names. She sighed, giggled, and said, "Go ahead, watch your movie. I'll get the dishes."

CHAPTER SIXTEEN

D aniel scooped up Diana from the recliner, and she snuggled closer. *This is not new.*

He kissed her forehead, lingered on a smear of blood on her cheek, then shook his head as though throwing off a dream.

Ducks in a row.

He carried her up the stairway and settled her onto her bed.

"Once every two months was enough for Mother," he whispered. He'd read about sleep-learning and brainwashing and started to go on about their mother's selection process that didn't bring questions to the doorstep. *Too late*, he thought, *she knows all that.* She'd already painted her room black on black to match her black quilt. Her plant sat on the bedstand instead of inside its special sun box. All of its needle-edged leaves were closed tight, with a bit of blood drying on their stems. He pulled the bedspread over her and said, "Now you're just a junkie who'll get us both killed."

"Tomorrow," she whispered.

"Tomorrow, what?"

"Paint your room. Paint kitchen."

"That's good," he said. "I'll work on the garage sheetrock."

She answered with a grunt and a snore.

Daniel hurried down the stairs, and Bill's arm twitched as he passed. He rushed into the garage, rummaged through tools to find his short-handled sledgehammer and a long survey stake. He hurried back to Bill, whose right hand clenched, unclenched.

Daniel placed the tip of the stake near the center of Bill's chest. The ravaged throat revealed fresh tissue already rebuilding deeper structures.

He must've been healthier than he looks.

Daniel took a deep, meditative breath, let it out, then slammed the stake through Bill's chest in three heavy, practiced strokes. Bill's eyelids snapped open, betrayed and unbelieving, and his hands scrabbled for a moment at the butt of the stake.

The struggle ended with a weak spasm and something unintelligible from the six-inch rip in his throat. Daniel rolled Bill's staked body inside the bloody tarp, dragged it into the garage and placed it into one of his shipping crates. He changed clothes, washed his face and hands in the workshop sink, then drove through clearing fog to find the boat haven.

CHAPTER SEVENTEEN

All their thrashing around had Tom tangled and sweaty in Marie's pink flannel sheets. He tried to free his cramping right leg, but Marie rolled on top and pinned him with a grin.

"Got you now, lawman!" she said. "What'cha gonna do about it?"

Tom wriggled his leg free enough to relieve the cramp. The rough callouses on his feet kept snagging in the soft material.

"Nothing, lady, I know when I'm beat." He put on his best pitiful face. "Just don't hurt me."

She nuzzled his neck and bit him playfully on the shoulder.

"Ah, Marie! Getting a little rough, are we?"

She nipped his other shoulder, gave him a full-body press and said, "Just warming up, my dear."

"What's next?" he asked. "The whip? Taxpaying public doesn't like to see damaged goods."

Marie lifted a corner of the sheet and slid sensuously and slowly down his body. From under the sheet she said, "None of those taxpayers better be looking at *this*!"

CHAPTER EIGHTEEN

Daniel parked the Mercedes next to C Dock at the boat haven where a row of scabby vehicles displayed their wounds of wind and salt air. Mist off the bay pressed the air close and damp. The tinkle and ring of rigging against masts played counterpoint with the foghorn in the bay. He stepped out of the mist and onto the pier with a bouquet of mixed flowers from the all-night Four Corners store on the highway. Jean met him halfway down the pier in her flower-print muumuu from last year's sail to Maui.

He handed over the bouquet. "Thanks for calling," he said. "You rescued me from a boring evening of construction cleanup and painting."

"These carnations are beautiful, and their perfume lasts forever. And tiger lilies! Thank you!"

The lights of the pier accented Jean's spatter of freckles, and Daniel envied Diana's freckles that broke up the glaring whiteness of their twin skin. Other freckled women he'd known wanted to get rid of them. The Matrix contrasted Diana's freckles more, the only thing she liked about it.

"The tiger lilies reminded me of you," he said.

She tilted her head with a quizzical look.

"The freckles," he said.

Jean laughed and said, "You thought of me. How sweet."

She sniffed the bouquet again and smiled. "There's always room for flowers on *Freedom*." She pointed to a mast three boats down. "That's my baby, my home. Forty-footer. She's old, but she made it to Maui and back."

Daniel offered his arm out of habit. She smiled, took his arm and led him to *Freedom*.

"This is nice," she said. "I'm really glad you came. You rescued me from something, too."

"What's that?"

"Sitting up all night alone, thinking of you."

Wildflower boxes lined the pier next to her moorage, and two more graced either side of the cabin door with the year's first daffodils. Jean stepped aboard the boat first and gave him a hand up. Wake from a freighter crossing the Strait made footing tricky. Daniel had never liked the water, but a sudden breeze pressed that shapeless dress tight against Jean's body, and he thought he might get used to it.

"You can see there's room for flowers," she said. "Large enough to live aboard, small enough for single-handing."

They were pressed close between the cabin and the rail. He smelled spar varnish, a whiff of diesel and plumeria perfume. Jean opened the cabin hatch and said, "Well, here she is, my humble home."

Daniel wanted to stay this close to Jean for another delicious moment, so he tallied the rest of the exterior: mast and automated rigging for the sails, helm, crab pot, coils of line.

"Nice sloop," he said. "Comfortable."

Jean looked skeptical. "You know a sloop from a ketch from a yawl?" she asked. "I took you for a big-city condo type." She put up her hand. "No offense. Boats are really just moveable condos."

Another boat wake threw Daniel off-balance. He snapped his hands up to catch himself and fell against Jean with both hands on her chest. He jerked them back as if burned, lost his balance again, and Jean caught him from falling backward onto the pier. They held each other, laughed, and kept holding.

"Hey, sailor," Jean said. "Maybe a drink will help those sea legs. Glass of wine below?"

They each held the same intense, deep-searching look that they had experienced in the hair studio.

"Yes," he said. "Yes, a wine would be perfect."

Her guided tour of the cabin didn't take long: a small chart table and communications area, a galley, hatchway to the head and hatchway to the forward berth. Radar, depth finder, and computer screens hung from the ceiling. Daniel sat at a dining table that doubled as a crew bunk while Jean produced glasses and a white wine.

"Plastic okay?" she asked. "Not elegant, but it's safer on a boat."

Daniel nodded. "Fine with me. I wish we'd had plastic when I was a kid … on boats, I mean."

Jean laughed. "Come on! You're about my age. We've had plastic on boats as long as I can remember, and I grew up on boats."

"So, you're a local?" he said, deflecting. "Here, let me get that for you." He gestured for the wine and corkscrew that she was holding and cautioned himself to be more careful about his history.

"Sailing was about our only way to get around when I was a kid," he said. "Our mother wouldn't travel any other way. She was lost on a solo sail to Mexico."

The latter wasn't true, but it slid easily off his tongue.

"I'm sorry!" Jean said, one hand pressing her chest. "Were you young?"

Daniel poured the wine. He hesitated at the question.

"I guess so," he said. "Yes, we would have been in high school if we had been normal."

They offered their glasses in a toast.

"Here's to normal," Daniel said.

"And here's to not," she answered. They touched glasses. "So, you were homeschooled, too?"

So began his new attraction to boats. *This will require some research*, he thought, and began his well-practiced story of his family's "allergy" and his need to remain inside all day. Jean refilled their glasses.

"So, how many people get this sun allergy?" she asked. "I've never heard of it before. Except in vampire movies, of course. And I know I saw your reflection in the mirror at Marie's, so *that* can't be it."

"Erythropoietic protoporphyria," he said. "Some call it 'sun poisoning.' Maybe one in a half-million gets it as bad as my sister." He finished his wine and Jean poured him another.

"Do people die of this?" she asked. "'Poisoning' sounds much worse than 'sunburn.'"

"A while back, the German Chancellor's wife committed suicide because of it. I worry about Diana. Radiation from a TV or computer screen gives her a burn. We used to go out to late movies, but she won't even do that anymore. Movies were her only way to see the daylight world."

Jean handed Daniel an afghan blanket and picked up their glasses.

"It's turned into a nice night since the rain stopped," she said. "Let's go up on deck." She picked up a large Pendleton blanket and two dry cushions with native killer whale motifs.

They cuddled up under the blanket on the cushions in the cockpit. An ornately carved raven formed the tip of the tiller. She leaned against the tiller, he relaxed against her warmth. Both watched a cloud bank drift to reveal the dipper part of the Big Dipper.

"I haven't stayed up and talked all night since college," Jean said.

"What did you study?"

"Nursing," she said, and laughed. "I finished, too, but ... I don't know. Too many sick people all wanting me to make it better. I'd probably make a terrible mom. Boat work got me through college, and I actually liked it. You, BioCosmetologist, must've gone to college. How'd you manage with your allergy? If it's a genetic thing, maybe it can be treated."

He sniffed a change in the air and thought, *It's coming. Maybe an hour left.*

"I went to a few colleges, and a couple of trade schools, all at night, of course." He savored his sip of wine. "I thought 'virus' when virus studies came out. Then I thought genetic because it's just us. Night access to that level of expertise and equipment ... not like taking Bio 101 at the community college." He sighed. "Still curious, though. I like learning new things."

"Like what?"

The morning chill inched up his spine.

"Engineering, sculpture, biochemistry. All night school or correspondence—easier now with internet. I'm working on something now that would make a great desalinator for coastal communities. An Israeli investor is interested at a scale I'm not prepared to match. Yet."

"Would it work on a boat?" Jean asked. "I want one, but they're *so* expensive!"

Daniel looked apprehensively at the eastern sky and felt grayness pressing the back of the Cascades.

"My prototype is like a small kitchen appliance. You're welcome to try it out on the boat. Maybe you'd like to see my workshop sometime? I won't quite have it set up tomorrow. Everything will still be a mess."

"I'd love that," she said, "messy or not. I'd like to meet your sister, too."

Daniel set his empty glass aside and nodded toward the mountains. "I have to go—daylight's coming. I need to get back and check on Diana." He stood and pulled Jean into a hug. "Why don't you come out tomorrow night? We can have dinner, look at the desalinator—"

"Check out your etchings?"

She kissed Daniel lightly and softly.

He laughed and kissed her back, resisting the song of life calling through her lips.

"Yes, etchings."

Another kiss, then he walked quickly to his car without looking back to where she stood, facing east, into danger.

CHAPTER NINETEEN

Marie woke up with a start when her alarm went off at 8:00 AM instead of seven.

Omigod! The kids are late for school and Jean's coming for a tint at nine!

Tom's side of the bed was empty, but his shoes waited under the chair that held his uniform coat and hat. She heard water running downstairs and threw on her bathrobe to investigate.

Tom stood at the sink washing breakfast dishes, trying to master whistling Roy Orbison's "Pretty Woman." No kids in sight. Marie felt dizzy from her rush downstairs and disoriented from oversleeping.

"What's going on?" she asked. "Where are the kids?"

He shut off the water and toweled his hands, then grabbed her in a hug.

"Kids are fed, clothed, teeth brushed, and at school. James was uncommunicative, Lucy chatty. She must've memorized that movie last night because she recited most of it."

She held him at arm's length for a good look.

"Who *are* you?" She looked around the kitchen. "And you cleaned up our mess from last night?"

"I'm the guy who reset your alarm," he said. "You were so conked out I thought you deserved a little more shut-eye. Breakfast?"

"Just coffee," she said. "I didn't clean the shop yesterday before or after our little party, and Jean's coming for a tint at nine."

He put an arm around her waist and guided her to the coffeepot where he poured them both a cup. "I can fix something while you sweep your shop."

Marie shook her head and carried her cup to the bathroom. "I have to get ready for Jean. Maybe lunch?" She shut the bathroom door.

Tom raised his voice so she could hear. "For the lowdown on the muck salesman, you mean?"

"I feel a little weak in the knees," she said.

Tom tossed the towel onto the counter, raised his cup in a toast and said, "Praise the Lord."

He checked his phone and found that his day off was now a day on. His patrolman called in sick for the second time in a week. The kid was the mayor's nephew and scored day shift with minimal experience.

"He's not getting more experience calling in sick," Tom muttered. Through the bathroom door he said, "I have to go to work. Maybe see you for lunch." All he heard back was the shower.

He didn't have time to go to his place to change clothes or shower. He thought of slipping in with Marie, but that would become more than a shower and neither of them had time right now. Lack of sleep caught up with him when he pulled up at the foot of City Dock beside the station. Instead of going right inside, he leaned against the rail and watched the boats out on the water. A dozen or so fished the mid-channel bank, and he wanted to be there. Cindy, the department's receptionist and sometime dispatcher, parked beside him and stood with him at the rail.

"Is Mark out there today?" she asked.

"Yep," Tom said. "He's the bright yellow boat in the middle. *Fishkiller.*"

She nudged him with an elbow. "When was the last time you fished with your brother?"

"A month before we pulled that insurance guy's Navigator out of the drink."

"You must be in withdrawal," she said.

Tom shrugged, rubbed his eyes. "A lousy month, in general."

They walked to the station door and Cindy asked, "No clue at all on that adjustor guy?"

"Nope. He was a loner. Like a transient, only rich." He opened the door for her. "He was from Portland, so they're covering that end. Most likely the car was stolen and dumped up here. Putting out the word to the homeless guys to speak up if anybody new has a tent in the woods."

Cindy walked inside but Tom held the door and kept talking, more to himself than to her.

"His bank account was wiped but no credit cards used. No unusual phone records. Not a trace."

Cindy sat behind the counter and turned on her computer. She adjusted the volume on the radio and tested her microphone. Tom signed the log sheet.

"FBI says there's never 'not a trace,'" Cindy said. "Maybe he's just fine with his cash and doesn't want to be found."

"Maybe," Tom said. "But if that's the case, our adjustor leased his car, then drove it into the bay. If he's not dead, he'll wish he was when I catch up with him."

"What makes you think he's dead?"

"A feeling," he said. He rubbed his eyes again. "Transients come through town every day. No matter what people think, they never leave without a word to somebody. Without a trace. There's always *something* … His credit cards had ten thousand in cash withdrawals he could've taken, but he didn't."

"If the adjustor didn't do it, then maybe the killer car thief will hit somebody here," she said, her eyes wide.

"Don't even say that," Tom said. "Besides, you've been reading murder mysteries again."

Cindy's lips turned to a pout. "*Hmph.* Don't mean I can't be right."

Tom leaned on the counter and stared past her through the window to the boats on the water.

"Transients get pickup work. If the guy's smart, he'll hold off flashing a lot of money and get some work as a cover until things quiet down." He spoke more to himself than to Cindy. "I checked out all of the building permits in the city for the past month. New guys weren't seen on any of those jobs." To Cindy he said, "Get me the permits for the county."

"The county is the sheriff's jurisdiction," she said.

"No kidding. I'll be darned. Well, as short-handed as he is, he shouldn't mind me doing some of his footwork, should he?"

"Just trying to keep you out of trouble."

Tom slapped the counter, louder than he'd intended, and startled Cindy.

"I'm a *cop* for Chrissakes! I make my *living* on trouble."

"Okay, okay!" she said, and waved him away from the counter. "Don't be a grouch about it!"

Tom headed for the door, then turned to say, "Tell the chief I'm at the courthouse. I'll get the permits myself." He strode to the cruiser and yanked open the door.

"Wouldn't want anybody around here to get in *trouble!*"

He took one last look at the boats on the water, shook his head and drove off.

CHAPTER TWENTY

Marie snapped on her rubber gloves and pulled her tint tray over to Jean, relaxing in the chair. She had two cancellations this morning because the rain had rolled in.

"They said, 'What's the point of getting my hair done and going out into the rain?'" Marie said. "Does no one in the Northwest own an umbrella?"

Jean laughed. "Maybe your business plan should partner with someone who sells those little purse-sized umbrellas. You could loan them, rent them, tack them onto the bill." She opened the top of her purse on the floor. "Ta-da! Teeny umbrella, four bucks!"

Marie changed the subject. "You asked for his number, *and* ...?"

Jean blushed her telltale blush and put her hands over her mouth. Behind her hands she mumbled, "Speak no evil."

Marie put on her shocked face. "You little hussy, you."

"Hah! Who's the hussy?" she asked. "I saw a patrol car in your driveway at daybreak on my way to breakfast. Have an emergency? Besides, you gave me his number, what did you expect?"

Marie mixed the color agent to a darker shade of red. Jean's gray no longer hid within her thin, reddish hair.

"I expected a report. Please begin."

Jean sighed, leaned back for the shampoo and closed her eyes.

"He's an insomniac, too," she said. "We didn't do anything but drink wine and tea and watch the stars. Well, clouds. Going to his place for dinner."

"Yeah, right, 'watch the stars,'" Marie said. "And I'm Mother Teresa. Going to his place ... shouldn't you go someplace public first?"

"What's he going to do, seduce me? Besides, his sister will be there to chaperone, of all the damned luck. What's the matter?"

Marie pinched the bridge of her nose and swayed a bit. She caught the arm of Jean's chair to steady herself.

"Nothing," Marie said. "Headache, a little queasy. I warmed up a piece of garlic bread for breakfast, didn't agree with me."

Jean made a wry face. "I love garlic bread, but not for breakfast." She shuddered. "No wonder you don't feel good."

Marie rolled Jean's chair up to the shampoo sink. "How do *you* feel?" she asked. "After the pack treatment, I mean."

"Great! What little sleep I got was wild dreams, honey, and I mean *wild*! I still look ten years younger in the daylight. How do you think I feel?"

Marie mustered some enthusiasm and soaked Jean's hair with the sprayer.

"Great. That's great. That's what this business is all about."

James walked in wearing his work clothes.

"Hi, Mom. Hi, Jean. I forgot it was teacher prep day for us. Do you have any work for me? I still need a hundred and twelve dollars for Art Camp."

"I don't, honey, Maybe Jean has something for you."

"Sorry, James," Jean said. "I sold the *Vulgarette* yesterday morning and I'm between projects myself."

Jean turned to Marie. "What about Daniel? They're doing all that work on their place at the bluff. I recommended Alice for the landscaping. Maybe she could use James out there with her."

James straightened to his tallest and said, "I rode my bike out there when it was abandoned. That's a huge job. Alice definitely will need some muscle."

Marie winked at Jean.

"I guess that leaves you out, toothpick."

James wasn't flustered.

"Mom, please! Lucy's bad enough. I can lift a *lot* more than Alice."

Marie said, "If you can lift the garbage out of here and out of the house, then sweep the walk, I'll give you a buck."

"Oh, wow, gee!" he said. "Like, a whole dollar? Gosh!"

"Then you only have a hundred and eleven dollars to go," she said. "Your choice."

James shrugged, and without saying anything more he carried the nearly empty garbage can outside.

"I've got to find something for him to do," Marie said. "He's going to drive me crazy, and I don't have money just to hand over to him."

She toweled off Jean's hair and set up the back of the chair.

"I'll ask around the boat haven," Jean said. "Whatever I find will be grunt work."

"Fine!" Marie said. "Keep him out of my hair. And tired."

She ran her dryer to take up the extra moisture in Jean's hair and showed her the color mix.

"What do you think of this? Not much darker. More highlights."

"I like it," Jean said. "Maybe if I darken my hair my skin will get the hint and I won't burn so much when I'm on the water. Next to Daniel's skin, I'm almost as native as Alice."

Marie sopped on cotton balls full of color and sponged off the excess. "It won't be hugely dramatic, but if it talks your skin into a darker tone, let me know. Opens up a whole new line of work."

Jean dozed while Marie finished up. Marie hummed a tune she couldn't name and averted her face from the color fumes that aggravated her headache. She turned Jean's chair to face the mirror and asked, "Okay?"

Jean flounced her hair, turned her head back and forth and said, "It's great! Maybe next week a little trim?"

She fished some bills out of her purse and set them next to the cash register. "How about lunch for a tip? I don't have anything on deck today except dinner with Daniel."

"I can't. Morning people cancelled but from noon I'm booked. Tom's taking me and the kids to dinner if he doesn't have to work late. How about tomorrow?"

"So you can get another goo salesman report?" Jean asked.

"Maybe."

"I'll see if Alice can join us," Jean said. "She's calling Daniel today about landscaping. I'll bet she gets the job."

"She looked pretty hot last night," Marie said. "Maybe she and the sister ...?"

Jean shook her head.

"I don't know," she said. "He's pretty classy in an old-school way. His sister probably is, too. Alice always wears those baggy overalls. She should feminize a little. And accessorize. Even if she's ..."

"Meow!" Marie said. "She owns a *landscaping* business. How do you accessorize for that? Gravel earrings?"

"Well," Jean said, "she has an art degree. Things represent other things." She tapped her lips and continued, "Technically, diamonds *are* gravel."

"Call me art blind, call me greedy," Marie said, with an eye-roll. "I'll take the diamonds."

Jean started to say something but stopped.

"What?"

Jean reddened from her chest to her hairline and cleared her throat. "Well. Speaking of diamonds, has Tom—?"

"We're *friends*!" Marie interrupted, louder than she'd meant. She felt her own face flush. "Sorry. I had a bad marriage, and Tom's hardly dated. Ever. So we don't talk about that."

"What *do* you talk about?"

"Fishing," Marie said. "And the kids. Movies. And food. We like food."

"Wow. Underwhelming. I would've thought you'd talk about your clients."

"Oh," Marie said, and laughed. "You mean *you*? Are you accusing me of violating stylist/client privilege?"

Jean hesitated, hand on the doorknob. "Is 'stylist/client privilege' a thing?"

Marie waved it off. "No, but he doesn't like talking about people he's arrested, so I try not to get too gossipy about clients. You and Alice, however, are fair game."

CHAPTER TWENTY-ONE

D aniel unfurled his blackout blinds just in time to head off dawn's feeble smirk behind the Cascades. He had to find and block the few occasional flickers of light that knifed through the untrimmed edges of siding. He pulled on an extra-long-sleeved shirt, Laplander hat, veterinarian's gloves, and welder's glasses. He slowly turned a circle, arms extended, and stopped when he felt a tingle on his nose, lips and chin. He returned a few degrees, back a couple, then chalked an arrow on the concrete between his feet. He covered himself nose to chin with a blue shop-towel bandana.

"Can't blame him, working alone," he told himself. "Lifting that sheathing up there by himself, then holding, securing, nailing it off ..."

He cut several 6-inch strips from a roll of roofing paper, pulled a ladder to the east wall and felt for the gap up by the sill plate.

"Not bad, not even a quarter inch."

Wind whined against the eaves and slipped through the gap. Daniel stapled up the thick, black strips but kept his gear on, just in case the paper failed behind his back. Workbench, rolling tool chest, double sink and stacks of plastic crates awaited new cabinets against the north wall. A half-dozen sixty-gallon, blue plastic barrels lined up against the house-side wall. Four plywood shipping crates, each seven feet long, two feet wide and a foot deep were stacked next to the utility room door. Bill the Odd-Jobs Man's truck dripped oil onto the clean concrete in front of the barrels. He'd tarped Bill's truck and backed the Mercedes wagon right next to it, leaving himself barely enough room to work.

He could think undistracted in a workshop, lab, or studio alone. Passing as other among others consumed his attention on any job.

Lots of humans pass as "normal" humans, like high-functioning autistics.

He'd met several autistics in nearly empty night labs across the country. To a person they likened their situation to nerve-jangling, full-time, onstage improv. Anxiety and insufficient food exhausted him at home. Diana's deliberate devolution, his own weakening against a buffet of temptation at work and their mutual cabin fever led to the greatest string of mistakes in their very long lives.

How to think our way out of this? he wondered. Sometimes she heard him when he wondered.

He pulled down the top crate and set the lid aside. The armature of heavy wire welded to a stainless steel, snap-out, three-legged base and his bulky protective clothing made wrestling it out of the crate a struggle. Daniel laid the framework onto the tarp next to Bill, who lay on his side with the cedar stake through-and-through his chest, Hawaiian shirt and all.

He shook his head at the shirt. "Northwesters!"

No sign of granulation in the bluish-white lips of the wound, no pinking. Daniel selected the reciprocating saw from his workbench and nipped off the ends of Bill's stake at the shirt buttons and the back. He tossed them into the scrap wood barrel. A large scoop dangled from the lip of the next barrel, and he dipped out about a half-liter of gray powder to encircle the dripping oil under the truck. The oil turned the gray powder into a lime green, taffy-like plastic where they touched. Daniel slid a stock-watering trough next to Bill and scooped in ten liters of gray powder. He brought the sink hose over and slowly added water, mixing with a round-nosed trowel. This mixture also turned green, a "Hunter Green" like his choice for the kitchen. With mixing, it textured like wet clay.

Next full moon and low tide, he thought, *clay strata should show up in the bluff face.* He preferred local clays, when available. They added indigenous flavor to his work.

He turned to the opportunity to clean up after Diana. The art part. Creation.

At least she did her own disposal last time.

He grumbled to himself about the dead Proxy.

I had to thaw him enough to stake him.

He was back there in the freezer when that cop knocked on the window!

Just two days after the Portland proxy's disappearance, that midnight radio wacko from Pahrump identified an insurance adjustor's mysterious fate in Oregon as "… another alien abduction." Daniel tuned in every night, awaiting radio wacko's inevitable confirmation of the goth girl's "… genuine spontaneous human combustion."

He dragged Bill to the wire-and-rebar frame and secured him into place.

Organic, he thought, with a nod. *Non-GMO.*

With considerable effort, he wrestled Bill upright, gripping the frame at Bill's chest, looking him right in the eye.

"Who's in there now, Bill?" He patted the dead man's cheek. "Nobody?"

Daniel adjusted Bill's head to open the pale gashes and tears in his neck, head almost severed with vertebrae visible. Hands into empty claws chest-high.

Scare ALL the children, Bill!

Daniel reached into his Mercedes and hit "play" on Mozart's *Requiem* at full volume. He lifted a bloody wallet and phone from Bill's pants pocket. He held the phone like it might bite him, pulled out the battery and chip, then smashed the rest with his hammer.

Careless, careless, careless Diana!

He used his acetylene torch to melt the chip and debris like he'd done with the ex-Proxy's. He turned back to his new Empty and slathered his quick-drying mud from Bill's feet to the top of the framework. He left an opening around Bill's eyes for the transformative sunlight that would bake the mold from the inside.

"Ah, Bill, you never looked so pretty!"

Daniel heard something through the music and turned it down.

Doorbell!

His security monitor revealed a cop at the front door. The night cop who gave him directions.

Shit! he thought, then he pressed the "Talk" button and said, "One moment! Be right there!"

He flicked mud off his gloves, rinsed his hands in the sink then adjusted his hat, gloves and goggles to go into the house and answer the door.

The day was cloudy, but Daniel was overwhelmed by the glare that framed Tom Aldrich in the doorway. Even with his goggles in place he had to cover his eyes with his gloves.

"Please come in," he said. "Hurry! Please hurry!"

Tom took a cautious step over the threshold, unsettled by Daniel's Road Warrior getup and the gloved hand pulling on his sleeve. Tom barely squeezed through the half-open doorway before Daniel slammed the door shut. The room was as close to coal mine dark as Tom had ever seen, so he stayed put in front of the door, hand on his weapon. Daniel switched on the light and raised his goggles to his forehead.

"Thank you for hurrying," he said. "No time to explain. I'm severely allergic to sunlight."

He unwrapped his face, took off his hat and gloves, and offered a handshake.

Tom hesitated and took in the heavy blackout curtain covering the large picture window in the back wall. A fringe of blue drapery stuck out from the bottom of the curtain. The walls were a shiny, dark blue with some vividly colored abstract paintings, or Asian writing, leaning against them, ready to be hung.

"Sorry, Officer," Daniel said, still extending a hand. "You caught me in my workshop."

Tom shook the offered hand and studied the man's face for malice. The gaze was steady, hand cold, handshake firm and not lingering. "I'm Sergeant Aldrich," he said. "I believe we've met?"

"Yes, I remember you. I'm Daniel. Thanks for the directions. I was very tired from the drive." Daniel gestured toward the dining room. "Can I get you some coffee?"

"No, thanks," Tom said. "I can't stay." He looked closer at Daniel's face. "You got quite a burn there. You couldn't get that on a day like today."

Daniel touched his nose and forehead. "Yes. That's why the gloves, goggles, blackout blinds. My sister is even more allergic than I. She won't leave her room until well after sunset." He peeled back his sleeves to reveal lumpy red welts. "A little burn on the nose, but it triggers these itching hives all over. I can take it for a little while. For my sister, it could be fatal."

Tom said, "That's pretty inconvenient, with your remodel work." He ran a hand over the shiny blue wall. "Real enamel," he said. "Everything's usually latex these days."

"Enamel doesn't gather dust like latex does," Daniel said. "My sister likes how it sets off the paintings, and it's easier to keep clean. Won't you have a seat?" He swept a hand toward the couch.

Tom shook his head. "No, thanks." He lifted a photo from his shirt pocket. "Ever see this guy?

Daniel controlled the surprise he felt at the sight of the adjustor, his ex-Proxy. He accepted the photo with both hands and studied it carefully without a trace of emotion.

"No, I don't believe so," he said. "What has he done?"

"Well, somehow he managed to disappear in Oregon but drive his car into the bay a couple of miles from here. Salmon fishermen snagged it. He was an insurance adjustor, so I thought maybe he'd been out here on business. I'm checking all the building permits, just in case."

Daniel's first thought was that his new Darkest Knight had made a fatal mistake already. He handed back the photo.

"We got our insurance in Seattle," he said. "But we haven't put in a claim. No reason to send out an adjustor for us."

Tom pocketed the photo. "I thought it was worth checking," he said. "I can let myself out if you want, so you don't get more hives." He turned to go, then changed his mind. "Maybe he stopped for directions?"

"You're our first visitor since we arrived," Daniel said. "We're pretty out-of-the-way."

"Right," Tom said. "Thanks."

He walked to the door and hesitated while Daniel put on his hat, goggles, gloves and scarf.

"Oh, have you hired any transient labor? People passing through who need a few bucks or a meal? We get a lot of those in town."

Daniel shook his head. "I hire only licensed local contractors and am only getting started. I'll be sure to check on any subs they hire and give you a list. I forgot … the PODs with our belongings came with two workmen to help unload, but they were both black, and the guy in your photo is white."

"Alright, that's fine." He waved a dismissive hand. "Thanks for your time—"

Daniel interrupted, trying to look like a worried homeowner. "Do you think some homeless guy killed this insurance agent?"

"Adjustor," Tom corrected. "His brother in Seattle said he liked driving back roads. Could've run into anything, anywhere between here and Oregon. You don't have to see me out."

Daniel said, "Come by any time, Sergeant."

Tom hesitated again, hand on the doorknob.

"You're the goo salesman, right?"

"Goo? I don't ... oh, I see," Daniel said. A crease of frown formed between his eyebrows. "How'd you know—oh, of course, you're a police officer."

"Small town talk," Tom said. "I also hear you're a sculptor. Let me know when you have a show. Thanks again."

Tom let himself out, and Daniel let out the breath he'd been holding. He peeled off his gloves and looked toward the stairs, listened for Diana. Nothing. Then he put the gloves back on, shook his head and hurried back to his chore in the workshop.

He finished troweling his mixture over Bill and gave him a gargoyle head and shoulders. Daniel was exhausted, his skin and clothing stained with sweat, dirt, mud. He listened for stirrings from Diana upstairs. Still nothing. He donned an extra ski mask, adjusted his goggles, then opened the garage door. He dragged the trough outside, dumped the dregs beside the driveway, and rinsed the tools and trough. The rain had quit, so he used a barrel dolly to get the new Bill into the side yard daylight. Then, hurrying and out of breath, he closed himself inside the garage and rushed to the blacked-out kitchen. He stripped off his cover, scratched furiously at his hives, and removed one of his bags of charged Matrix from the refrigerator. His trembling hands had trouble measuring out exactly one cup of the blood-red goo into the top of his appliance. "Martini," he said. The green light winked on and he placed his martini glass under the spout. He washed his face and hands at the kitchen sink while blood pulsed into his glass.

CHAPTER TWENTY-TWO

J ean drove Alice and James out to Bluff Road just before sunset so they could meet Diana and talk business. Jean wanted the excuse to visit with Daniel in his home, but she was curious about his sister, as well.

How a man treats his sister says a lot about his relationship with women, she thought. She'd met too many bastards who'd revealed clues too late— kicked their dogs, swerved to the shoulder just to hit a raccoon, cursed their mothers, bullied sisters. Without her own kids, she was "Auntie" to James and Lucy. She liked James for being protective of his sister without being bossy. *He'll be a good one!*

James rode in the back, daydreaming out the window and bobbing to whatever streamed through his earbuds.

Alice made notes in her iPad as they approached the property and got out immediately when they parked. She shot a 360-degree series of the property in front of the house while Jean rang the doorbell and James kicked gravel into a pothole. The door opened just enough to squeeze through, but nobody was visible.

"Please, come in," Daniel said, too far back for them to see. "Excuse my appearance. I've been in the workshop."

Jean led the way as the three of them rushed through the doorway that slammed shut behind them. Daniel was just a dark figure in a dark room, only slightly lit by a red LED nightlight in the far hallway. One large picture window nearly filled the back wall, covered with a double layer of black fabric. Not one glimmer of the last of the sunset bled through.

Daniel flipped on a light and began stripping off his hat, ski mask, scarf, gloves. James took a step backwards, to the door.

"I hope I didn't scare you," Daniel said. He hugged Jean and shook hands with Alice and James. He told James, "You looked pretty pale, there. This is just my daylight getup."

James managed a nervous laugh and said, "I couldn't be as pale as you. Are you, like, albino?"

Daniel smiled. He'd heard that before. "Not quite albino," he said, and indicated his light brown hair. "Just pale. My sister, Diana, even more so."

As if on cue, Diana's bedroom door opened upstairs and she stood silhouetted in the backlight from her room, her body visible through her floor-length silk dress, the same green as her eyes. She appeared to glide down the stairs, those green eyes watching James's gaze watching her move. She also wore a white silk scarf at her neck and white gloves. She made quite a contrast when she stood next to Alice's baggy overalls and sweatshirt. Alice was more circumspect than James in her appraisal of Diana's body.

"Diana," Daniel said, "this is my friend, Jean. And her friends, Alice and …?"

"James," Jean filled in. "Son of Marie, who owns the hair studio that Daniel visited."

Diana didn't extend a hand. She offered Jean a curt nod with no eye contact, then smiled and offered a more gracious nod to Alice and James. "A pleasure," she said.

Jean felt a chill and rubbed her arms.

"Would you like some water?" Daniel asked. "Some tea or coffee?"

"I'd love some coffee," Jean said.

Alice said, "Nothing for me, thanks." She fidgeted with her iPad, eager to get to work.

James tried not to look like he was looking at Diana's figure. She was a little taller than James, and her nipples hardened in the cool room. She couldn't resist moving closer to tease him a little.

"James?" Daniel said.

James startled and just said, "What?"

Daniel said, "Sorry, we don't have any soda. I'll be sure to stock some if you'll be working here."

James shrugged. "It's okay. I'm only supposed to have one pop a day, and I had one for lunch."

Diana leaned closer, almost breathing in his ear. He felt something stir in his pants and shifted his stance.

"You say 'pop' out here instead of 'soda'?"

He started to speak but felt his voice tighten to a squeak. He cleared his throat and said, "Um, yeah. 'Pop.'"

Daniel clapped his hands and rubbed them together. "Well, Alice and Diana, you probably want to talk landscaping. Jean, care to join me in the kitchen?"

"Sure," she said, and flashed him a smile, "I can grind beans, or something."

Diana indicated the couch and said, "Please, have a seat." She sat between Alice and James, but closer to James. Diana noticed Alice's lips pressed into a line of disapproval.

Or jealousy? she thought. She considered that a promising sign.

James said, "Why does your couch face the wall?"

Diana laughed and patted his knee. He squirmed closer to the arm of the couch.

"It's a beautiful window looking across to Canada," she said. "Daniel seals it up for me every day because I'm violently allergic to sunlight. We can open it in a few minutes, if you'd like?"

"Nah," he said. "It's okay."

Diana turned to Alice. "Well," she asked, "what kind of landscaping do you do?"

"Heavy natural landscape is my specialty," Alice said. "Your allergy, it must be difficult for you ..."

Diana waved a dismissal. "One adjusts," she said. "But I can only visit our grounds at night. I like space to walk and large things easy to see. Not all that brush. Maybe big rocks among those trees."

"Boulders?" she asked. "How big is too big?"

Diana offered her first smile. "Yes, big boulders. Clear out that brush and ferns for walking paths. At the gate ... here." She stood and offered a hand up to Alice, then led her to a photograph on the wall behind them. "Here's what you see from above."

Alice examined the aerial photo of the property while Diana stood back, appraising Alice with an upraised eyebrow. James fidgeted on the couch, watching Diana watch Alice. Alice photographed the photo and made some notes on her iPad. "Most of the boulders around here are glacial erratics," she said. "Granite from Canada delivered by melting glaciers about twelve thousand years ago."

Diana feigned interest. "I didn't know that. You see what we have—trees and brush and ferns and gravel."

Alice turned to face Diana, excited and eyes glittering. "But what *great* trees!" she said. "Even a few of the last old growth in the county. Of course, they block some of the light to the house, which is good for your condition but might have resale consequences."

"I don't want to cut any of them," Diana said. "For shadow and privacy. I just want to walk among them at night without tripping."

The women shared a smile. "Great!" Alice said. "I hate cutting trees. I'd like to walk a bit before it's too dark now. Then back in the daylight for measurements and jobs for James. *Then* I can bring you a selection of lot plans and computer simulations for all four seasons. Then the rocks."

Diana stood closer, until they nearly shared breath. "How long for that?"

Alice needed the work but didn't want to seem eager. She felt light-headed when she held Diana's green-eyed gaze. She spoke in a near-whisper. "A week. James and I have to map and inventory, take some measurements ..."

Diana whispered back, "Just you two. Please, no more people. I require much privacy." She nodded toward the kitchen. "Not like my brother, the people person."

Daniel, re-swathed in his protective cocoon, strolled with Jean on a path just outside. The sun was down but aggravating light still reflected from the overcast. Through walls, insulation and several layers of enamel, Diana concentrated her hearing to catch their banter.

"You look like a caterpillar," Jean said. "Especially with those awesome goggles."

Daniel laughed a muffled laugh and took her hand. "Maybe you'll like the butterfly?"

"Maybe. Probably. Okay, for sure!"

In the living room, Alice said, "We can manage nicely, just us two. I can rent and handle the heavy equipment myself. We'll get James on the brush right away."

Daniel and Jean stopped under a huge cedar beside the driveway. He peeled back his muffler and ski mask and she kissed him in one swift move. He kissed back, hugging her close.

Diana paused in her conversation with Alice, cocked her head as though listening to a quiet conversation.

"Tomorrow, perhaps?" she asked.

"It'll take some shuffling," Alice said. "But, yes, James can make progress on the brush while I figure how to get the equipment in here with minimal damage. Right, James?"

James stood and nodded, still captivated by Diana. Neither woman looked his way.

"Yep," he said. "I mean … yes. Sure. No school tomorrow. I'll bring my Weed Eater."

Alice shook her head. "This heavy brush is too much for your Weed Eater. I put a sling blade in Jean's trunk with some other tools. Remind me to drop that off for you before we leave."

"What's a 'sling blade'?"

"Some say 'brush hook.' It's heavy and sharp, like those Scottish swords Lucy says you like."

James blushed and said, "Oh."

Diana reached out her hand and Alice met the handshake, lingered. Alice's hand came back slowly, her expression flushed, quizzical. James looked from one woman to the other and registered their mutual attraction with some disappointment. The movement in his jeans registered no disappointment at all. He noted no fangs in Diana's smile. Lucy asked him to look.

"Very good," Diana said. "You have family, Alice?" She held Alice's name into a soft hiss at the end.

"My parents," Alice said. "In eastern Washington. Yakima."

"Interesting word, 'Yakima.' Could be from anywhere. Anyone here in town?"

Alice shook her head. "Just Rascal, my cat. I'm pretty self-contained."

Diana threw a bitter look toward the shrouded window and the invisible couple beyond.

"I understand," she said. "I have a plant."

"A favorite plant?" Alice asked. "What kind of plant?"

Diana turned for the stairs and called over her shoulder, "Venus

Flytrap, a Black Star. Remember, I can't answer the door in daylight. Thank you for coming."

Alice and James waited for Jean beside her car in the driveway. James practiced swinging the blade through a clump of salal. Alice occupied the wait by sketching out some lot features nearest the house. Daniel and Jean strolled around the corner of the house, holding hands. Daniel carried most of his extra clothing, his face red and slightly swollen in the dusk.

"Hey, James," he said. "You can practice on that tangle between the house and the bluff. That's a mess."

James asked Alice, "How much time do we have right now?"

"I have a little more to sketch, lists to make. Go ahead, knock yourself out. I'll holler when we're ready."

Jean handed Alice her keys.

"Would you mind taking James back to town when you're ready?" she asked. "Daniel will give me a lift to the boat later."

Alice shrugged as though expecting this development. "Sure, no problem."

Jean looked exuberant. "Thanks! I just got a look at one of his weird sculptures—you don't mind me calling it 'weird,' do you?"

Daniel bowed slightly and said, "No other word would do."

"He's also invented a desalinator," she said. "Could be hot in the boat trades."

"That's great," Alice said. Her tone was flat and her body already leaned toward town.

A flicker of disappointment passed over Jean's face, then she revived her exuberance. "Anyway, I'll see you in town. Keep the keys, I have a spare."

"Good evening," Daniel said, and shook Alice's hand. "Thank you for coming. It means a lot to my sister." He waved to James who hacked at head-high salal at the back corner of the house. James registered no recognition, and Daniel took Jean's hand.

Alice spoke to Jean's retreating back. "I'll drop the keys at the boat haven."

Jean waved an acknowledgment without turning around. Alice looked on, uncomfortable without knowing why. She looked at the house and, in the darkness, made out a second-floor curtain slightly parted, no figure in sight. Daniel opened the front door for Jean, and when the door closed, Alice shuddered. She joined James at the back of the house where he already showed good progress.

"Let's get back," she said. "We'll get everything we need for the morning. I'll pay for your time today."

"Okay," James said. "Cool!" He set the blade against the house and donned his earbuds.

Back at the car, Alice asked, "Didn't Jean and the sister look a lot alike?"

James removed an earbud and said, "What?"

She shook her head. "Nothing," she said.

Alice paused several times in the long driveway to make notes and to take more pictures.

"I should've taken a picture with you and the blade," she said. "Your mother would love it."

James nodded, but she couldn't tell if he agreed with her or with his music.

CHAPTER TWENTY-THREE

M arie stood at her kitchen sink, sipping a glass of ice water. Her stomach hadn't settled much after her disagreement with the garlic bread.

Maybe I should call Doc Rowe for an appointment.

She hadn't been able to afford health insurance since she opened the shop. Doc Rowe was willing to trade haircuts for the kids' school physicals, which helped, but Doc Rowe was running out of hair.

Lucy came in from the shop with an armload of towels.

"Mom! What's this?" She pointed out large, brownish-red stains on three towels from the shop hamper. "This looks like blood! I didn't want to wash them in case they stain."

Marie picked up one of the towels, sniffed it, rubbed it between her fingers.

"Hmm," she said. "Nobody's been bleeding. Sure looks like blood." She sniffed again. "Maybe it was that face-pack goo. It turned red."

She dampened the towel under cold water, rubbed the stain and rinsed it away.

"Cold water works. At least it's not permanent." She gave it back to Lucy. "Just use the cold-water setting."

"Gross!" Lucy said.

Marie sighed. Something churned in her belly. "Hey, I know ... leave that laundry for later. I'm not feeling well and don't have an appointment for two hours. Let's just sit on the couch and watch a movie. Want to watch *Bride of Dracula* again?"

"Sure!" Lucy said. "Can I nuke some popcorn? It won't spoil my dinner."

Marie stood too fast and slapped a hand over her mouth.

"Oh, no ... I'm going to be ..."

She ran for the bathroom.

"Pregnant?" Lucy finished.

James clumped into the kitchen in his work boots and hurried to the refrigerator.

"Who's pregnant?" he asked. "You, squirt?"

He pulled out a quart of milk and a plate of leftovers.

"Nobody, nosey. How was work with Alice?"

James gulped down half of the milk and scooped a mouthful of cold spaghetti out of the Tupperware.

Lucy started the popcorn in the microwave, frowned at James and poured herself a glass of milk before he drank it all.

"Cool," he said. He spoke around another mouthful of cold spaghetti. "Alice paid me for doing like almost nothing today. And she says this job will go a while, so camp's in the bag."

"What about those night people? Any vampire signs?" She lifted the large silver cross she wore whenever she watched vampire movies.

"Signs like what?" he asked. "They're just weird, is all."

The popcorn finished popping so she pulled it from the microwave.

"Weird like baby sacrifices in the full moon?"

"Didn't see any babies or any sacrifices," he said. "Besides, I think that's Satanists." He wiped the Tupperware clean with a slice of bread and reached for the popcorn. "She's really hot. Like, *hot* hot. They're allergic to the sun, so, yeah, probably vampires. No fangs, though. Just normal teeth."

Lucy grabbed back the popcorn bag and mimicked James by stuffing her mouth full. Bits of popcorn flecked her mouth when she said, "Better carry a silver bullet, just in case."

He scooped a huge handful of popcorn into his mouth and mumbled, "That's werewolves, Runt."

She smiled her popcorny smile and said, "Silver garlic, then."

James shook his head and tossed the Tupperware into the sink. He picked up Lucy's glass of milk and slugged down half.

"Hey!" she said. "That's mine!" She saved the last of her milk and took the remaining popcorn to the living room for her movie.

James passed Marie on his way upstairs and she said, "Whew, stinky boy! You need a shower!"

"That's where I'm going *Mom*! Geez!"

He clomped upstairs and she asked Lucy, "What's with him?"

Lucy offered her the popcorn and said, "That vampire woman, she's 'like, hot.'" She used air quotes for emphasis.

Marie said, "I don't want to think about it," and started their movie.

CHAPTER TWENTY-FOUR

Tom's microwave dinged and he removed his bowl of steaming leftover spaghetti to his desk, next to his diet ginger ale, paper towel, and plastic fork. Cindy chatted on the phone with her girlfriend and the radio behind them blared chatter between two fire units looking for an address. He pulled out a stack of building permits to review.

Tom grumbled at the firefighters on the radio, "Jesus, dudes, just look for smoke!"

He dug into the hot spaghetti, so hot he could barely keep it in his mouth. He breathed hard to cool it and Cindy said, "You okay over there?"

"Hot-hot!" He sloshed a drink of ginger ale around his wad of hot food just as a disheveled man in his early sixties walked in and strode to Tom's desk.

"Tom?"

Cave Dave was one of Tom's most stubborn homeless customers. Dave preferred the raw outdoors, but sometimes sought shelter in a barn or shed, and sometimes the owner didn't like that. Cave Dave knew every officer in the county.

"Cave Dave?" Tom said and took another bite. "Hot!" He sluiced another wash of pop, swallowed and said, "To what do I owe this honor?"

Cave Dave said, "Bill stole my tarp."

Tom thumbed the building permits, not really listening.

"Bill who?"

"Odd-Jobs Bill. Stole my tarp. Rain's coming."

Tom set his paperwork aside and Dave took a seat in a chair beside the desk. He always looked squirmy and uncomfortable indoors, even in a good chair.

Tom said, "Never knew Bill to steal before. What makes you think he stole your tarp?"

"He borrowed it for a job," Dave said. "'A quick job,' he said. I been to his trailer place every day for two days. He's gone. Truck's gone. Bill stole my tarp."

Tom's interest perked right up.

"What job?"

"Something in the county," Dave said. "Out on the bluff. Had to be done in two days and it's two days. No Bill. No tarp. Therefore ..."

"Therefore, maybe the job ran overtime and he's still borrowing. Anything else missing at Bill's besides your tarp and his truck?"

Dave shook his head. "Bill don't have nothing to miss. He's been missing water and electricity for about twenty years. Hauls barrels of water from his jobs. Showers in the boat haven with the yacht folks."

"Did you look around inside his trailer?"

Dave cast a sideways look in case Tom was going cop on him. Tom waited.

"Okay, yeah. I took a little snooze on his couch while I waited. Short little couch. All his stuff's there except my tarp. About five thousand moldy sci-fi books."

"How long was that 'little snooze,' exactly?"

Dave folded his hands on the tabletop and looked at them.

"Okay. Two days."

Tom sat up straight and pushed his food aside. "Didn't come back at all?"

"He didn't wake me up if he did."

Tom slid his note pad and pen over and asked, "Where you holed up now, in case I find this disappearing tarp. At Bill's?"

"Nah, too small, too indoory, too moldy in there." Dave sneezed twice. "The Fogfarm. Gray's letting me stay in his shop. It's big but I'm getting cramped-feeling again, you know? Gotta be on the move pretty soon."

Dave finally met Tom's gaze, and Tom asked, "Think you'll be on the move out of town this time, Dave?"

Dave shot him a sorrowful look. "Now, Tom, you know those sheriffs out there got no sense of humors. You-all treat me fair here in town, and you know I'm no trouble."

Tom waved his stack of building permits at Dave.

"All these newcomers don't know that, Dave. One of them's liable to take a shot at you one of these days. I don't want that, the paperwork's a bitch. You don't want that. Stay out at Gray's, there's woods out there."

Dave stood and brushed the chair off behind him. "I'll be at Gray's until I get my tarp. Or until the rain's back and I get work to buy another. Appreciate your time."

Dave shook Tom's hand and left. Tom stuck his fork into his spaghetti, then pushed it aside. He ran a hand through his hair, drummed his fingers on his desktop, then put on his hat and stood to go.

"Cindy, I'm going out to Odd-Job Bill's to look around. I'll be on portable."

"That's in the county," Cindy said. "You running for sheriff now?"

"I know where the city limits are," he said. "Like I said, I'll be on portable."

His hand was on the doorknob when Cindy said, "Did you forget? You have skateboarders in court in half an hour."

"Shit!" Tom took off his hat, slammed it onto his desk and sat down.

"Well, don't take it out on me," Cindy said. "You're the grouch who wrote the tickets."

CHAPTER TWENTY-FIVE

Marie rolled Alice's chair back to the shampoo sink and wet her hair with the sprayer.

"How about something new today?" Marie asked. "Some color? Permanent?"

Alice enjoyed the head massage with her eyes closed and said, "You ask that every time. I just want it trimmed, don't need anything fancy."

Marie switched to the shampoo and continued the massage.

"What if it's a treat? You know, for free?"

Alice huffed and tensed, a little indignant. "I'm employed, you know. I *can* pay."

"I know you can," Marie said, and patted Alice's shoulder. "You say that every time, too. That's not the point. It's a treat. I like to treat my friends, especially when it's a quiet day like today."

She rinsed Alice's hair, wrapped it in a towel and rolled her to the workstation.

"James says you two got a good start out there," Marie said. "Too bad he had school today, he really likes the work."

"He's a good worker. Doesn't have to gab or get instruction twice. I'll give Diana the final layout tonight and bring in equipment tomorrow."

The shop bell tinkled and Jean strode in looking flushed, big smile, eyes a-glitter. She stood beside Alice's chair without a word, still smiling.

"Well?" Marie asked

"Well?" Alice asked.

Jean put a hand to her cheek, batted her eyes, and continued smiling.

Alice let out a groan and said, "You didn't!"

Jean patted Alice's wet hair and said, "Oh, but I did. And then he did. And then we ..."

Alice put up her hand to stop Jean's narration. "Please," she said. "Don't whip me with details. Aren't you afraid of ... you know ... catching something? You just met him. You don't know where he—"

Jean snapped open her handbag and pulled out a string of a half-dozen condoms.

"Ta-da!"

Alice made a wry face. "I don't like those things."

Marie combed Alice's hair down to the straps of her overalls and judged her cut line.

"You know that we know that you don't need them, right?" Marie asked. She held a mirror so Alice could see the back, pinched a section of hair about three fingers above the shoulders and asked, "How about here?"

"Fine."

"Did you even look?"

Jean sat in the other shop chair and rolled it closer. "I *like* men," she said. "And I like this one a lot!"

Alice groaned again. "You mean you like a lot of men. And you don't know that much about me. I do all right."

Marie shot a "watch this" glance at Jean and said, "Oh, yeah? When was the last time?"

Alice wriggled in her chair and Marie squeezed her shoulders to settle her down.

"I'm not going to blab to you two about my sex life. Really!"

Jean laughed and said, "You'd blab if you had something to blab!"

Marie focused on snipping Alice's hair and changed the subject. "So, Jean, tell us what we don't know about Daniel. You aren't going to screw me out of another free facial, are you?"

"Okay. First, he's gorgeous!"

Both Marie and Alice said, "We know that!"

"Okay, okay," Jean said. "He makes the goo in a lab in his workshop. Not everything's completely set up yet. He makes these weird sculptures out of special dirt. They sell in Europe and Seattle for a bundle. He invents things, like the desalinator. That'll be a money-maker that I'd like to get in on."

"Dirt sculptures?" Marie asked. "What in the world are dirt sculptures?"

Jean settled into her chair like she was holding court. "The dirt is special. Mixed with water and heated it looks like fired clay, but he says it's a plastic. They're crude and grotesque like some chainsaw gargoyles. He gets twenty-five thousand for one, after the gallery fee. That's as much as I got for selling *Vulgarette*!"

"What about the sister?"

Jean shook her head. "Maybe Alice should tell you."

Alice didn't reply.

"Okay, she's as gorgeous as he is. They're twins; he says she's the oldest. I haven't seen her again since we met. I got the feeling that she disapproved of me, didn't you, Alice?"

Alice said, "Definitely cold to Jean."

"She actually gave me the creeps. The look I got when I went to the kitchen with Daniel? Severe. But she sure liked *Alice*." Jean drew out Alice's name for emphasis.

Alice blushed. "They're all like that at first. They think I'll work cheaper if we're pals."

Marie said, "Hold still, I'm almost done. You squirm worse than the kids." She turned to Jean and asked, "Bedrooms?"

Alice put up a hand again. "Wait! Wait a minute! If you're going to give a blow-by-blow account—"

Jean and Marie started laughing.

"Blow-by-blow!" Jean said and laughed even harder. "Listen to her!"

Alice blushed even more and rolled her eyes. "You know what I mean. I don't like hearing that stuff. I don't kiss and tell."

Jean said, "You've got to kiss a lot of frogs to find your prince." She aimed a heavy wink at Alice. "Or princess."

Marie finished Alice's trim and held up the mirror for a final nod. "And you've found your prince?" she asked.

Jean turned serious. "Wow," she said. "You know me, Ms. Never-Ask-A-Last-Name. But I think so. I really like this one. Those green eyes!"

"Like his sister's," Alice said. "Startling. I'll bet he's got women strung from here to Hamburg. Or wherever he's from."

"California," Jean said.

"Figures," Alice said, with a huff.

"He's invited me out again for dinner," Jean said. "Diana said she'd like to go over your plans tonight." She nudged Alice and stage-whispered, "Maybe she's ... you know ..."

"Oh, just stop!" Alice said.

Marie took off Alice's cape and finished a brush-off. Alice counted out the money and a tip and said, "I'll call her when I get home. You two. Really!"

CHAPTER TWENTY-SIX

Diana squeezed out the last pink drop from the gray slop in the bottom of a plastic bag. She tossed the bag and mass into a stainless-steel bucket and returned it to the fridge. Behind her, Daniel prepared a large salad.

"How can you stand it?" she asked.

Daniel shook his head. "It passes the time, and I like their food. You make an unnecessary mess of *our* food. What's with that?"

Diana threw her head back, hissed like a cat and said, "It's a curse, this thing called Time. Anyway, either I eat or I sleep. Hunting passes the time, but I tired of merely passing time long, long ago."

He saw her hunger back already, heard the dangerous edge in her voice.

"Your eating style—" he began.

"Brings a little excitement into my very boring life," she said. "How could I stand it otherwise, locked up in this tomb or some other. Even my workouts and painting are boring for me now."

"We still haven't unloaded your gym equipment from the garage," he said. "Maybe that'll help."

In a dramatic flourish of frustration, Diana threw her hands in the air. "I'm tired of working out for something to do when I don't need it." She slapped her tight belly with both hands for emphasis.

"It's not a tomb," Daniel insisted. He strained to speak in his calm voice. "It's a very comfortable house. I'd like to stay in it for a while. You can't keep killing people—"

"Don't lecture me!" she snapped. "I like the personal touch. Besides, I don't kill them. *You* kill them."

Daniel slammed his knife onto the cutting board and turned to face her. Her expression shifted between defiance and despair, and back. He reached out and gripped her shoulders. Her expression just got colder.

"What I kill is not human when you're done with it," he said, trying for calm. "If they lived through their first glimpse of daylight, if someone didn't stake them, they'd be out there hunting our back yard. We'd be staked in our beds or trapped outside some sunny afternoon ourselves. Or worse."

He realized he was gripping her too tight, but she offered no complaint. Just a steady gaze and defiant thinning of her lips. He couldn't endure her piercing stare and let go of her shoulders. He turned back to his dinner preparations, cleared his throat and added, "Behave yourself tonight. I like this one."

In her own measured voice she said, "Don't give me orders. After all, I'm the oldest."

"I've told you before, twelve minutes in two hundred years doesn't carry a lot of weight with me."

"It better," she warned, "or I'll drain your little tart like a garden hose."

Daniel pretended to ignore her as he chopped a handful of mushrooms. Her kills were too close together, too careless, and lately her tone had become dangerous. He'd begun to worry about his own safety. His sleep was increasingly restless. He'd felt more comfortable during his brief time with Jean in the cabin of her boat than in his own bed.

Diana flicked a piece of lettuce, picked it up and took a bite. Immediately she spat it into the sink.

"Ugh. How can you gag that stuff down? Worse than the swamp rats we had to settle for when we were kids."

"It's an acquired taste," he said, "like civilization. Besides, *they* like it. Maybe you need a friend. Or a pet."

"I have Robert," she said. She ran her finger under the spout of the appliance and licked a drop off her finger. "He gets me."

"He's a plant!"

"Exactly. He knows how I feel."

CHAPTER TWENTY-SEVEN

Marie finished up a story to Tom at the dinner table as the kids sat down to eat.

"So, I told her, 'Why should I settle for hamburger when I have steak at home?'" She patted Tom's hand. "Steak. That's you, Tom."

James mumbled, "Spare me." He made a finger-down-the-throat gesture to Lucy.

Tom lifted an eyebrow but otherwise ignored him.

"Thank you, *dear*," Tom said. He threw a glance at James for emphasis. "And thanks for the invite to dinner. Going out doesn't compare with your cooking."

Marie passed the salad and exaggerated a smile in response. James repeated his "gag me" gesture. She continued her story as they helped themselves.

"Then all of a sudden I saw all these raw meat images: a pool of bloody hamburger thawing in the sink, a raw steak bleeding on a white china plate ..." She shuddered.

"Gross!" Lucy said.

"Can we just eat?" James asked. "I'm like starving here."

Tom said, "You don't have to explain it to me, I *like* vegetarian lasagna. Just don't spare the garlic bread." He passed the lasagna platter to James and said, "Is that *really* starving, or just *like* starving?"

"Probably *like* starving," Lucy said. "He's not *that* skinny."

James made a sarcastic face at Lucy and focused on his plate. Tom tore off two pieces of bread and handed one to Marie. Marie dipped her garlic bread into her tomato sauce, took a tentative bite and chewed carefully. Tom and Lucy talked about an obnoxious new substitute at school. Marie swallowed and immediately felt ill. The small dinner noises and the conversation faded to a high-pitched ringing in her ears and turmoil in her belly. She dropped her bread onto her plate, kicked her chair back from the table and raced to the bathroom.

Tom and the kids looked at each other in surprise. James just shrugged and dug into his food. Lucy held Tom's gaze for a moment, almost said something, then returned to her dinner.

"What?" Tom said.

Lucy shook her head and didn't look up. "Nothing."

CHAPTER TWENTY-EIGHT

Diana was lounging on the living room couch, studying the lights across the water, when her cellphone beeped. Daniel and Jean chatted in the dining room over the clink of dinnerware. Occasional bursts of laughter punctuated the buzz of their conversation.

"Alice, yes, thank you for calling," Diana said. She used her most diplomatic tone. "How nice of Jean to give you my message. I hoped you might come out tonight to see the place as I do. Is that a bother? Of course, I'll pay you for your time."

Alice lived in an apartment over her shop, overlooking her garden and nursery. Her cozy apartment held minimalist Ikea furniture on birds-eye maple floors cluttered with seedling trays, plant starts and potted trees. She curled up on her futon, warm and comfortable in her jeans and her "Save the Trees" sweatshirt. She sipped at a full glass of merlot.

"Actually, that would be handy for me, too," Alice said. "I can set some stakes tonight for the heavy equipment tomorrow. James has school tomorrow, so he can't come out until afternoon."

Diana smiled her perfect smile and glanced in the direction of the dining room where the couple enjoyed their dinner and each other. The smile became imperfect.

"Perfect!" she said. "Would an hour from now be too late for you? Good. I'll meet you in the driveway in an hour."

Diana hung up and stood with a coy, girlish look that reflected from her window. She cocked her head and told herself, "A woman. Well. I hope she trimmed her nails."

Daniel and Jean retired to Daniel's bedroom and sat in the nook of his large bay window. This window, too, overlooked the water and lights on the other side.

"What do you think?" he asked.

"When I see the lights?"

"Yes."

She took a moment, leaning against him, his arm around her waist. "There's still a new world out there. Canada is so close, but so different. I've traded a few boats up there. Every time our economy tanks, I dream of starting over up there."

Daniel nuzzled her neck. "Does it make you think of food?"

"Food?" she asked. "Not really. Why?"

He glanced toward Diana's room. "Nothing. That town, they see us, too. From the air at night we look like two crab pincers, and the crab has a grab on the night."

Diana shifted her position from listening at his door when she heard the rustling of sheets and the dropping of clothes.

And I have a grab on you! Diana thought.

She couldn't resist and turned back to the bedroom door in time to hear Jean say, "My boat is stocked, packed, and the tanks are full."

Daniel said, "Yes, I'd like that. But I have to care for my sister, and she's just settling in here. Maybe one night we could sail over and back."

"No problem," Jean said. "You just name the night. I love sailing at night. It's as close as you can get to being on a starship."

Diana heard kissing, heavy breathing, then boatlike movement on the bed. She straightened up, tapped her teeth in thought, then slipped down the hallway to her own room.

Meanwhile, Alice set her backpack onto her kitchen table and loaded it with her computer, cellphone, note pad, drawing pad. She zipped it up, then unzipped it to add her flashlight and a fresh bottle of merlot. She emptied her glass and shouldered the backpack, then retrieved her mountain bike from the shop. She pedaled down the road, her reflectors flashing rhythmically on her spokes.

The faint winking of a red channel marker in the Strait matched the flash of reflectors on Alice's bicycle's approach in the driveway. Diana stepped out of her housedress completely naked and searched her closet until she found her painting overalls, like Alice's, with some dark blotches and stains on them. She stepped into the overalls, cinched up the straps so they fell just right on her breasts, then checked her pockets for several lengths of white nylon rope. She paced her window like an albino panther before going downstairs to head off the doorbell.

CHAPTER TWENTY-NINE

Marie couldn't face dinner after her episode in the bathroom, so she hugged Tom at the table and excused herself to go to bed.

"I'm really sorry," she said. "That's the second time in a row that garlic bread got to me. Usually I have to keep from eating half the loaf." She put a hand on his shoulder as he started to get up. "Please, finish your dinner. Maybe I just need to lie down for a bit."

Tom and the kids glanced at each other and James said, "It's okay, Mom. We'll clean up."

Tom saw that James was serious. *No teen sarcasm!* he thought. "I'll wash if Lucy'll dry," Tom said. "I don't know where everything goes, so maybe James can put them away."

"I like drying," Lucy said. "I don't like scraping."

James helped himself to another piece of lasagna and said nothing.

No sarcasm, Tom thought, *but just a pinch of sullen.*

After the dishes were done, Tom carried a glass of water up to Marie. A soft little snore stuttered from her open mouth. He kissed her forehead and left the water on the bedstand. He still had a night's work ahead, on his own time.

The old travel trailer at the end of Odd-Jobs Bill's driveway wore more green algae and moss than faded blue paint. He parked well back from the cinder block steps to the door and unclipped his heavy flashlight from under the dash. He preferred the flashlight to his nightstick in a one-on-one. He worked his way back and forth, examining the ground and brush. Thanks to an hour of heavy rain earlier, the only fresh tracks were his own. At the door, he saw no marks around the knob or lock. He held the knob at its shaft, turned it easily and the door swung out.

Cave Dave didn't break in, at least. Like most old-timers around Salish Landing, Bill never locked his door.

Tom stood in the doorway for a moment and swept the area behind him with the light. The headlights of every derelict car that Bill ever owned reflected back at him from the blackberry tangle that made up his front yard. An outhouse leaned away from the blackberries, pushed by the vines to a risky tilt. He turned his light inside the trailer but stayed in the doorway. He didn't like surprises.

His search was mechanical. He kept the wall to his left and worked his way to the back bedroom. Many small piles of t-shirts and sweatshirts littered the unmade bed and the floor. Bill actually had a method—clothes on the bed were clean, those on the floor, dirty. The tiny trailer bathroom was insulated with science fiction paperbacks along three walls. The tub held two scrawny, dead pot plants in a bed of old *Scientific Americans*, a beat-up rocking chair replaced the toilet, a kerosene lamp sat in the sink. Back down the hallway and into the living area Tom found books on shelves, the coffee table, countertops, kitchen table, inside cupboards and on the arms of the couch. Cave Dave was right about the mold.

The kitchen table held a kerosene lamp, the mantle type, and an open pizza box with a few moldy crumbs and a helping of mouse turds. He lit the lamp carefully and switched off his flashlight. He opened the door to Bill's old-fashioned icebox and found two Rainier beers in tallboy cans, some bread with green mold and cheese with gray mold, a pack of slimy, unidentifiable vegetables and some spoiled hamburger.

"Jesus!" he said and slammed the door. "Gag a maggot!"

He picked up the top book on the kitchen table, handling it only by the edges and between his palms. If anything went bad with the sheriff, he wanted plausible deniability, like politicians. It was a cheap manual that somebody made on a copy machine: *What To Do If You're Captured By Aliens.*

Kiss your ass goodbye, he thought.

He started a more detailed search, looking for receipts, and absent-mindedly sang the children's song "Oh where have you been, Billy Boy, Billy Boy? Oh where have you been, charming Billy …?"

One of the kitchen drawers held a shoebox with mail in it, mail addressed to "Odd-Jobs Bill" at a PO Box in town. Tom wrote down the PO Box on his notepad and circled the zip code.

"In town," he mumbled. "My jurisdiction. Thank you, Bill." It was a thin argument for searching the place without a warrant, but the only one he had.

"Door was open," he argued to himself. It didn't help.

Tom sat at the table and thumbed through Bill's mail by kerosene lamplight, handling the paper only by the edges.

CHAPTER THIRTY

A lice pedaled up the dark driveway to the dark house and leaned her bike against Jean's car. She unhooked the bungee cords around her bike rack, dropped an armload of survey stakes and ran her fingers through tangled hair. Usually she wore a helmet, but the rain had stopped, and she wanted to feel the wind.

"Hello!" right beside her ear startled Alice. She stumbled backwards, fell against Jean's car and knocked her head on the trunk. "Dammit!"

A hand out of nowhere caught Alice's arm and helped her scramble upright.

"Omigod!" Alice blurted. She leaned against the car to catch her breath and managed a nervous laugh. "Oh, you scared me! It's so quiet out here. I didn't hear you at all!"

Diana rested a hand on Alice's shoulder, then gave her a hug. "I'm so sorry! Yes, it's quiet. I get used to moving quietly so I don't disturb the animals. Are you all right now?"

Alice took a deep breath, blew it out, then laughed again.

"I'm fine. I lost a couple of years, but I'm fine."

Diana slipped the hand on Alice's shoulder under the middle of her backpack and guided her away from the car toward a path that entered the woods in front of the house.

"Well," Diana said, "I hope I can make it up to you sometime."

Alice waved it off. "It's all right, really."

"The quiet outside at night is rejuvenating, I've found," Diana said. "Shall we?"

She moved her hand under the backpack, and Alice didn't shrug it off. She was attracted to Diana, but very cautious in her intimate relationships. Business with the public required discretion in a small community.

"There's a clear spot up here," Diana said. "We can get a good look back at the house. You'll see the rest of the brush I'd like taken out."

Alice's vision adjusted to the dark on her ride down the driveway, but now, with no moon, the landscape swathed its ebony shapes in dark air.

"And the boulders?" Alice asked. "Where to put those? I can get some so big that they come one to a truck."

"Excellent!" Diana said. "I'd like them up here, in the clearing. In a circle, like those stone ruins back in England. You've seen those?"

Diana's voice was soft, lulling. Alice shrugged off her backpack to lean closer. Out here, in the night chill, she felt cozy in Diana's company.

"Only in movies and books," Alice said. "I've seen the Stonehenge replica down on the Columbia River. I was there for ... for ..."

"Yes?" Diana whispered in her ear. "What were you there for?"

"An eclipse," Alice said. "A beautiful eclipse with snow glittering on the stones."

"Sounds lovely," Diana whispered. Then she hooked her arm into Alice's and led her into the clearing. "So, here we are. We'll need a compass to orient our great stones properly."

Alice said, "I have GPS on my phone. It's in my backpack."

The only sounds were their breathing, cheek to cheek, and a breeze creaking nearby branches. Their arms moved around each other's waists. Alice tried to concentrate on business, but she couldn't shake the mental fog that settled on her with Diana so close, her breath so warm.

"Once we clear the brush we'll see how we're going to get a backhoe in here with the rock. That may be tricky getting through all the trees."

Diana turned around and put both hands up to Alice's cheeks; her close, green gaze rendered Alice nearly breathless. She didn't resist Diana's surprisingly tender kiss, and neither woman closed her eyes. Alice kissed her back, warming quickly and suddenly eager. It had been a long time. They undressed each other in a fumbling scramble, then lay on the long, damp grass in a blur of body on body.

Finally, they pulled apart and Alice said, "My whole body's tingling!"

"The night's not over," Diana said. She nuzzled Alice's neck, lingered there, sucking.

"Are you giving me a hickey?" Alice asked, with a chuckle. "I like it."

Diana said, "I'm glad." Then she ripped into Alice's neck with a hiss and a growl. One hand clamped on Alice's airway, so all she got out was one shrill, broken-off fragment of a scream.

In the house, Daniel sat bolt upright in bed. His sensitive hearing caught Alice's shriek, and his startle reflex woke Jean.

"What is it?" she asked. "Is something wrong?"

Daniel's expression hardened as he stared at the window, then softened when he realized Jean was beside him. He patted her thigh, kissed her neck.

"No," he said. "Nothing. Just a bad dream."

He glanced again at the window before he turned back to Jean. She kissed him, then sat up on the edge of the bed.

"I hate to say it, but I have to go."

Daniel felt a jolt of fear hit his belly. He couldn't let Jean out there, not right now. "Can't you stay the rest of the night?"

Jean turned and said, "I'll be honest with you."

Daniel swept back her hair and held her gaze with his most sincere expression. "Please do."

"Your sister makes me nervous," she said. "I don't think she likes me very much."

Jean stood and started dressing in the dark.

Daniel said, "Diana needs me. She worries that you'll steal me away and leave her helpless."

"Well, then. Maybe after she gets to know me better."

Daniel said, "That means I'll get to know *you* better."

"You already know me pretty well," she said. "Body-wise, I mean. How about dinner on the boat tonight?"

Daniel got up and pulled on his clothes. "I'd like that," he said. "Today I'm painting the kitchen and this room while Diana unpacks the last from the PODs, then I'm sheetrocking the shop. I'm scheduled to demonstrate the Matrix at the Hot Cuts shop across town tonight. Is ten too late?"

"Ten is good," Jean said. "Don't use up all your energy on housework, and I won't tell Marie you're over there seducing her competition."

They kissed again, and over Jean's shoulder, out the bedroom window, Daniel saw two dark figures, one dragging another into the trees at the edge of the clearing.

"Let me walk you out," he said.

"Oh, a gentleman!"

At the car, Jean saw the survey stakes and said, "Alice must've dropped these."

Daniel said, "I'll pick them up and make sure she gets them."

Jean started the car and in the headlights Daniel caught a glimpse of reflectors and a wheel lying back in the brush. He hoped that Jean backed out without noticing. He sniffed the air, sniffed again, looked out at the clearing and growled. He kicked the stakes and returned to the house where he hesitated, studied the eastern horizon, then hurried inside and slammed the door.

CHAPTER THIRTY-ONE

The shriek of a rusty hinge and the slam of the trailer door in the wind woke Tom from a sound sleep at Odd-Job Bill's cluttered table. He noted the drool on his notebook where he'd written Bill's box number. He folded lumber yard and hardware store receipts, with delivery to a familiar address on Bluff Road, and slipped them into his notebook. Tom rubbed his face and checked his watch.

"Just enough time for a shower," he mumbled.

He shuffled to the door, half-awake, gripped the shaft of the knob again and slammed it tight.

Nothing about this felt good. On the way home, he checked his phone for Bill's site on Handyman.com and noted his cell phone number. He thought he might try for Bill's phone records, but his probable cause for a warrant was still mighty thin. He suspected where it would lead and hoped he wasn't just paranoid. He resolved to ask James about goings-on at the end of Bluff Road. He needed to talk with Marie about his sudden uneasiness around letting James work out there alone.

Chief's on vacation for another week, he thought. *We were already two men short when he hired the mayor's fuckwit nephew, which makes us three men short.*

Usually he liked working alone, but now he worried that he couldn't cover the daily bullshit while he felt something big hovering close on the horizon.

Starting with that insurance adjustor. And his car leased in Portland collecting starfish a mile from Bluff Road. Not a casual afternoon drive.

He thought back to the goo salesman's truck with Mercedes wagon in tow, both with Washington plates, arriving at Bluff Road just after the adjustor's car was found. They'd clearly had a long drive after buying the place sight unseen. The Mandells had disappeared from Bluff Road not long before, so far without family or a trace, supposedly on a trip to San Francisco. No credit cards used on the trip. No record of arrival. Bank account emptied. House auction process accelerated, in Tom's opinion, even though the sheriff never closed the missing persons case.

Maybe Cindy's mystery novel habit is rubbing off.

He pulled into his parking spot beside his apartment and listened to the engine ping for a moment. He'd turned off his cell on his clandestine trip to Odd-Job Bill's and switched it on. He had a message from Marie.

"I woke up feeling much better," she said. "Thank you for the water and for cleanup. If it's not too late when you get this, slip off your shoes and come on by."

Another depressed sunrise tried to elbow its way through the overcast. He sighed and headed for the shower.

Sorry, Marie, he texted. *Too late, this time.*

CHAPTER THIRTY-TWO

Alice's eyes itched ferociously as the gray dawn washed to a searing pink. She itched ferociously but couldn't move her arms to get at the worst spots on her neck. She could barely lift her head to see the ripped flesh of her breasts, claw marks across her belly. A white nylon rope secured her wrists and legs to nearby trees. Soul-chilling terror rose at the premeditation of the rope and at her feeble, useless struggles. She was naked, spread-eagled, bone cold even though the skin at her wrists reddened and bubbled in the faint light of dawn. She screamed, but all that came out was a deep, rasping cough, like a lung-shot bear. The slashes on her chest and belly curled out, exposed their gaping slashes to the burgeoning light, and those edges, too, began to bubble. The clearing around her, trampled grass soaked in blood and branches snapped, mirrored the force of a battle she barely remembered.

The skin on her face and hands burned with the light, bone-cold damp replaced now with a flame-thrower. She twitched and squirmed, cringed and thrashed, but the burning intensified. Alice screamed again, but only a dry hiss escaped the gashes in her throat. Her skin blackened and peeled. She couldn't keep her eyes open against the acid sunlight, but her struggles freed one of her wrists as the skin peeled off. She slapped and thrashed as her body bubbled and burned with a *hiss*.

CHAPTER THIRTY-THREE

A slice of pale calf's liver plopped into hot grease with a *hiss* and Marie shook the pan so it wouldn't stick. Lucy popped a container of biscuit mix against the counter.

"Do we *have* to have liver?" Lucy asked. "It looks gross."

"We women need the iron," she said. "It builds stamina."

James shredded lettuce at the table and said, "I don't need *that* much stamina!"

"Slice some onions," Marie said. "I need them now. You're going to school, skateboarding, bicycling, cutting and hauling brush for Alice—you need stamina."

"So what do onions do?" he asked.

Marie smiled without turning around. "They make you cry. More men need to cry."

"Oh, please."

Lucy laid out little pucks of biscuit dough on the cookie sheet. "Crying makes you sensitive," she said. "Girls like sensitive."

"Oh, please," James repeated. "Mom, I've called Alice twice for a ride and she doesn't pick up. Her phone's not taking messages, either. She's supposed to give me a ride."

Marie tried flipping the liver but only folded it and splashed hot oil on her wrist. "Damn!" She ran cold water over her wrist and felt in the drawer for a spatula. "I can't take you because I have two late clients. I won't be done before dark."

He started peeling the onion and stopped. "This is one dull knife." A dramatic hand to the forehead. "I can't work in these conditions."

Lucy giggled and pushed the biscuit pucks into the oven.

"What?" James said.

"Nothing," Lucy said. "Sometimes you're just funny."

Marie turned the liver. "Onions!" she ordered.

James grumbled something too low to hear. He peeled and sliced the onion remarkably fast for using a dull knife. "Here. Can I get a ride *back* from the bluff if I ride my bike? You got mad last week when—"

"When he rode to Sequim to see that girl and couldn't make it back," Lucy said.

"That was because he overdid it and wanted me to come get him when I was busy," Marie said. "Set the table."

"Busy with *Tom*," Lucy added.

"With a *client*. And I didn't want him on Discovery Road at night on a bike." Marie shook the spatula at Lucy. "Set the table, Missy."

James slid the lettuce and onion trimmings into the compost. "Alice has all the tools," he said. "How do I know if they're out there?"

Marie set the liver and onions on a platter in the center of the table.

Lucy made a face at the ring of blood around the edges. "Mom, really?"

"Really," she answered. "At least five decent bites. And James, Alice is efficient. I'm sure she's been out there all day hauling rock and probably thought of everything."

James fetched the milk and glasses, and they all sat. Marie served each of them a piece of liver.

"You could call out there," she told James. "His card's on my desk."

"Mom! I don't want to call people I don't know. I'll just bike out."

Marie sighed and sat back in her chair. "My day always goes better when we sit together for dinner."

"Amen!" Lucy said. "Where's Tom?"

Marie sighed again. "Working. He works too much. Now eat." She turned to James and said, "The bluffs aren't that far. It's okay if you don't ride back after dark."

James utilized his sarcastic voice. "Don't worry. I won't ever call for a ride again."

Marie dropped her fork and looked him in the eye. "Hey! You know what I mean. Call if it's an emergency. Just think ahead so there won't be an emergency. Okay?"

James busied himself with finishing his food as quickly as possible, then rinsed his plate in the sink.

"If she's not out there, I'll be right back. If it gets dark—"

"You can hitch a ride with the bride of Dracula!" Lucy said, and laughed. "Here!"

Lucy took off her large silver cross necklace and placed it around his neck. James rolled his eyes at Marie.

"You'll thank me later," Lucy said. "You look *sooo* hip-hop!"

Marie clinked her glass with a fork and said, "Stop harassing your brother. Finish your dinner and start cleaning your room."

Lucy sat back and crossed her arms. "What will you pay me?"

Marie pinched the bridge of her nose for patience. "You just got dinner. You might get breakfast. Don't push your luck. Now eat!"

"I ate my five bites!"

Marie thought that those were the smallest five bites ever taken, but she chose not to engage. She stabbed the remaining liver off Lucy's plate and dropped it onto her own.

"Go!" she said, "and leave me in peace!"

Lucy giggled and said, "But we didn't have any peas."

"Just go!"

James was already gone.

CHAPTER THIRTY-FOUR

Diana paced in front of their living room drapes in a slow, languid daze. Deep scratches tattooed her arms and hands in red stripes and dotted them with tiny red quarter-moons. "Flight of the Valkyries" pounded from her sound system, and she licked a slash in her wrist that faded with every pass of her tongue. She wore an ankle-length white caftan of Egyptian cotton that Daniel gave her for their birthday in San Francisco. Her attention was on a toy, a glass bird with overlong wings balanced atop a glass post on their coffee table. The bird turned and dipped in response to the wind currents Diana stirred up as she moved. Their mother got it from a carnival glass-blower passing through New Mexico in a swap for one of her psychic readings. The graceful, hypnotic bird was one of only two relics from their mother that Diana hadn't burned or broken. The other was her mother's ivory-handled penknife for milking her cattle.

Daniel followed her movements while he answered the phone, then he stiffened and slammed the device onto the counter. His hand trembled. He brushed back his hair in anger and frustration.

When the phone hit the table, Diana stopped pacing, blinked twice and cooed, "Something wrong, dear brother? I smell something wrong."

Daniel hurried into the living room and planted himself in front of her nose-to-nose.

"The woman at the hair salon. Jean's friend. Asking if their friend Alice is here working on your project."

Diana met his gaze and held it. "And?"

"And I want to know what happened out there last night. Obviously, you've fed yourself. Will the law come knocking again? Who was it?"

She engaged her cooing voice again. "Maybe it was just a deer. Bambi."

"Don't play with me, Diana!" A fleck of spit hit her cheek. "You hate animals!"

Diana snapped out of her lethargy, wiped her cheek with her sleeve and bumped her forehead into his without breaking her wide-eyed gaze.

"And *you* hate *us*!" she growled. "You hate what our parents made us. You love your pitiful humans. You eat like them, think like them, *mingle* with them. Get it through your head, Brother. Your studies, your experiments will never make you human! You can get away with fucking them, but you can never live with them because *they can't know*!"

She emphasized with three jabs to his chest with a finger, then backed away. She closed her eyes, draped her arms over his shoulders and leaned her cheek against his chest. He stood still and said nothing.

"Our mother was human at one time," she said. "But you and I were born this way. How can you miss something you never had?"

Daniel sighed and put an arm around her shoulder. "Their lives are so much simpler."

She snorted a laugh. "Simple, yes. They work work work until they die die die. Fascinating. Boring. *Forget* them! Forget this sailboat woman. You and I—"

Daniel pushed her to arm's length and held her shoulders. "I *like* Jean," he said. "Have you ever liked anyone? Even once?"

She smiled. "I like *you*."

"I don't think so," he said, and shook his head. "You need me for planning, proxies, IDs and cleanup."

"But I *don't* need that," she said. "I'm happy to live wild. You think you have to protect me, and that's touching, but it's your need, not mine."

"If you're going to kill Jean's friends, then we have serious trouble between us. What happened to the landscape woman?"

Diana pulled away, looking tired, her scratches just pink smears on her white skin. Her composure went cold and her expression, hard.

"*Trouble* between us?" She hissed the "us." "Will a stake come between us in my sleep someday?"

Daniel didn't falter. "I can smell her on your breath. Is she going to be trouble?"

She turned in a huff. "There was a time you would have licked her off my teeth." She walked to the stairs and waved a hand in the direction of the clearing.

"She's in the clearing. See for yourself, I've cleaned up after myself. Isn't that what you wanted?" She stopped partway up the stairs and, without turning around, said, "Okay. There's a bicycle and a backpack. *Your* business. I have painting to do." She cranked her Wagner full volume.

Daniel hurried to his workshop locker and pulled on his bulky sweat-shirt and jacket, his long rubber gloves, white ski mask and scarf. At the door he snapped on his hat with the ear flaps and his sunglasses. He rushed into glare too quickly for his eyes to adjust, even with the glasses. Momentarily disoriented, he nearly panicked before he could make out the gravel path between the tall cedars. His breathing became desperate as he beat through thick salal to the clearing.

He stood, stunned, catching his breath, and sized up signs of the considerable struggle. He found the gore-covered loops of white rope tied to trees across the way. He tracked a trail of clotted blood and tissue, and as he neared a clump of bushes, he heard high-pitched, fast, tortured wheezing. He shoved the brush aside and found a cowering, badly burned lump of animal.

"Alice?" It came out in a dry croak.

The lump that was Alice made one last effort to burrow under the brush, then stiffened and stopped breathing. He knelt and saw that she'd melted more than burned. The overcast and the brush slowed everything down, and it still had a way to go. He felt a wash of sadness and despair that he hadn't felt since their mother died, in agony and alone on the side of that New Mexico roadway.

With a great effort of will, Daniel dragged what was left of Alice back into a safe spot in the clearing. *More sun today*, he thought. *She'll go fast*. He gathered the loops of rope, scattered clothing and a backpack. After a long last look at the blackened, bubbling remains, he shuddered and turned away. Hives had started on his face and arms, so he had to hurry. He shook his head and whispered, "You didn't have to do that. You didn't have to do *that!*"

Daniel gathered the evidence in his arms and rushed down the path, searching for Alice's bicycle.

CHAPTER THIRTY-FIVE

Tom sat at his desk, notebook open, talking on the phone with Stacie at the lumber yard. Behind him, Cindy filed reports, opened and slammed file drawers. Tom ignored the radio chatter in the background.

"Ten gallons of blue, green, red, and black enamel?" he asked. "Isn't that a lot of enamel?"

Stacie said, "Yeah. And he specifically asked for real enamel, not that fake latex that's supposed to look like enamel. Cost more than twice as much but he said, 'Money's no object.' Not a line I've ever heard from Bill."

Tom underlined LUMBER YARD several times in his notebook.

"Does Bill have a license?" he asked. "You know, bonded and insured, all that?"

Stacie laughed. "Bill? Not a chance. He's cheap, he does good work, but I don't think he'd fill out a form to save his life."

Tom thanked her and leaned his chair onto its two back legs. He teetered there in thought, tapped his teeth with his pencil, and asked nobody in particular, "Why would somebody want ten gallons of enamel?"

Over her shoulder, Cindy said, "Maybe he's a potter."

Tom lowered his chair back into place and turned around. "What?"

Cindy said, "My brother's a potter. He did his whole mud room in several coats of enamel so it'd be easy to hose down. Maybe the guy who ordered the enamel—"

The phone rang, and Cindy answered. Tom stood, began to pace, and finished her sentence. "Does something really messy and needs easy cleanup. Even in his living room."

Emergency tones came over the radio and dispatch said, "Sixteen?"

Tom answered on his portable, "Sixteen."

"You have an injury accident at Washington and Water. Aid car en route. Time out: 1420."

Tom rolled his eyes, threw on his coat and hat and replied, "Roger. Washington and Water. ETA two minutes."

"1421, Sixteen. Be advised, fight in progress. Two males."

Tom shook his head, snagged a baton from the wall rack and an extra-heavy flashlight from the desk and hurried to the car.

CHAPTER THIRTY-SIX

James leaned his bicycle against the side of the garage, dropped his backpack and listened for Alice. No sound of work outside, and no sign of any heavy equipment or giant rocks.

Maybe she's sick, he thought.

He called for her and heard nothing back but wind and waves and the bell on the channel buoy. He walked to the back of the garage, the water side where Daniel had wanted some brush cleared. The sling blade leaned against the garage wall where James left it. "Lucky," he told himself. He could get some money made before dark.

He scraped and chopped the salal but pulled the scotch broom out by the roots because that's how his grandfather said to do it. He worked shirtless now that the weather had cleared, even though the breeze off the water was cold. Lucy's heavy silver cross banged his chest with each swing of the blade. He thought she was right, it *did* look hip-hop. He hoped for cool. He piled the brush to the side of the driveway, away from trees, in case the owners wanted it burned.

James finished the back of the property from the house to the edge of the bluff in about two hours. He retrieved a bottle of water from his backpack and slugged down half of it, took a couple of breaths and downed the rest. He dropped the backpack beside his bike, slung his shirt over his shoulder, walked around to the front door and rang the bell.

A female voice, faint, called from upstairs, "Come in! It's open!"

James stepped into the dark and hesitated. His eyes weren't adjusted yet, so he couldn't see anything but the crack of sunlight from the door.

"Hello?" he asked.

Diana called from upstairs, "Please close the door! I'm deathly allergic to sun." She clicked a switch and a dim, reddish light washed the room.

"Sorry," James called back, and slammed it shut behind him. "I forgot."

Diana appeared to float down the stairs in her long-sleeved, curve-hugging, cleavage-clinging blue dress. James knew staring was impolite, but he stared anyway. She knew her effect on him and enjoyed playing it out.

"I've finished the work Mr. Daniel had for me yesterday. Alice said today I could start on your walking trails, but I guess she's not here."

Diana stepped closer, enjoying his attention to her figure. She was still woozy and a little slow from Alice and was saving him for later.

"I don't have to start home for another hour," he said. "Maybe you or Mr. Daniel need something done?"

"Daniel is his first name," she said. "Mr. Daniel is his professional name. I don't know why. Do you remember me? I remember you, James."

His blush was even visible in the dim red light. "Diana." His voice cracked, so he cleared his throat and repeated, "Diana. Has Alice called or anything?"

She moved closer, nearly touching him. He took a step back.

"James, may I get you something. Soda? I mean, 'pop'?"

He was perspiring more heavily, not just from the work. His nervous hands clenched and unclenched.

"No ... no thank you," he said. "I just had some water. Is Mr. ... is Daniel here?"

She ignored his question and said, "You'd like to be paid, of course." She rested a hand on James's bare shoulder. He didn't know what to do about it, so he froze.

"Well, yes, ma'am. But Alice said she'd—"

"Diana, please. I'm not ma'am." She faked a sorrowful look. "Do I look that old?"

James said, "No, ma ... Diana. No, you don't look old at all."

She squeezed his shoulder. "What *do* I look like?"

Her other hand picked up the cross from his chest. She bent down to bite the cross and her breasts nearly spilled from her dress. She placed the cross carefully back on his chest, gave it a pat. "Genuine silver," she said. She stepped back and assumed a modeling pose.

"Wow," James said. His voice cracked again. "You look good. Totally. Really."

"You seem eager to get back to work," she said. "I won't keep you this time. Daniel's in his workshop. Through the kitchen, down the hall, through the laundry room. Careful of the fresh paint. I hope I'll see you again soon."

"Thanks, Miss ... thanks, Diana."

She'd already started up the stairs.

James entered the kitchen and realized he'd been clutching his cross. He glanced back at the living room, but she was gone. He lifted the cross, bit it where Diana bit it, then shook his head and smiled.

In the workshop, Daniel filled a shipping crate with packing material around one of his grotesque sculptures. He was preparing the lid when James walked in, slightly shaken by his encounter with Diana. The workshop was cold in spite of all the new insulation in the walls and ceiling, so he pulled on his sweatshirt. One LED worklight hung over Daniel and the crate, and a huge black tarp covered the inside of the garage door.

"Hello, James," Daniel said, and waved. "I'll be right with you. How did it go out back? All cleared up?"

"Yes, sir," James said. "All done. Did Alice call? She was supposed to be here." He stepped up to the shipping crate and said, "Wow! What's *that*?"

Daniel laughed. "Sculpture. Like it?"

James reached out and touched the ghastly face. The material looked jagged but the surface was smooth. "It's awesome scary." He sniffed at the giant eye-holes in the face. "Whew! It stinks!"

Daniel laughed again. "That's the best review I've ever received, thanks. It'll cure for another day or two, then I spray a resin inside that smells like fresh cedar." He turned back to the crate and said, "No, no one called today. Maybe she had other jobs to finish up."

James let Daniel finish nailing the lid on the crate and looked around the shop. *Much better than the shop at school,* he thought. Full metal and woodshop, arc welder, lathe, drill press. The ceramics kiln in the corner was larger than his school's. Another sculpture stood next to its crate, ready for shipping. He examined that one through its eye-holes and saw the welded framework under the ceramic-like finish. It didn't look easy.

"These things are cool! And you make these?"

"I do," Daniel said, and bowed. "There's a big demand for grotesque these days. A by-product of our politics, I believe."

"Who buys these?" James asked. "What do you call them?"

"I call them 'dirt sculptures,'" Daniel said. "Galleries call them 'Primitive Earthenware.' The main ingredient is local clay and a cement-like sand that brings out the rough yet fragile quality that I like. People think plastic, but it's simpler and cheaper."

Daniel dusted himself off and joined James in front of Bill.

James asked, "Do you get a lot of money for them? Am I not supposed to ask that?"

Daniel maneuvered them so that James's back was to Bill's pickup. Peeking out from under the tarp, the bottom of a bicycle wheel and reflector hung from the back.

"No secret," he said. "This one's going to a new gallery in Seattle. If it sells for what they're asking, my share will be fifteen thousand."

"Dollars?"

Daniel laughed again and slapped James on the shoulder. "Dollars. Are you interested in art? Or in money? If money, the sure thing's banking."

James felt excited, like he'd just got a good grade on a test, or something.

"I'm pretty good in art class," he said. "But all we do is like draw or paint. Nothing 3-D, except for a vase for Mom. School's kiln could fit inside yours. I'm like saving for Art Camp."

He felt comfortable with Daniel, and Daniel seemed comfortable with him.

"I went to several art schools when I was young," Daniel said. "Good art schools, too. But I learned my most valuable skills in cabinet and metal shops."

"What do you mean?"

Daniel indicated his equipment, waved a hand at the toolboxes and other tools hanging on the wall. "Once you learn what all those tools are *supposed* to do, you get an idea of what they *can* do. Artists are notorious for using the wrong tool for the wrong job to get the right effect."

James scuffed his shoe through some sawdust. "Would you teach me how to do this stuff?"

Daniel feigned indignation. "What! And give away my professional secrets?"

He glanced toward the door that led to the laundry room, thinking he heard something, then back to James, who looked disappointed.

"Just kidding!" Daniel said. "Look, I'm just starting a project that Jean thinks will sell to the boat crowd. There'll be some welding and metalwork that you could start on."

James bounced on his feet and blurted, "That would be so cool! Welding!"

Daniel cocked his head slightly, listening again at the laundry door. He patted James on the shoulder and led him to the side door. He took Odd-Job Bill's wallet out of his pocket.

"I have some computer work to do," he said. "I don't have chores for you right now. You did two hours today, right? Will this do?"

He pulled a twenty and a ten out of Bill's wallet and handed the money to James.

"Well … thanks!" James said. "This is great! But I thought Alice was supposed to pay me."

"I asked to borrow you for that strip in the back," he said. "She'll be fine with it. Now, you'll have to slip out fast—you know about our sun allergy, right? That's why everything's sealed up in here. Took me a couple of days to get it right."

Daniel picked up his carpenter's apron, threw it over his head and shoulders, then turned his back. "Okay, go!"

"Thanks again!" James said, then opened the door as little as possible and rushed through.

Daniel unclenched his teeth and listened for the sounds of James getting on his bike. He stared for a long time at the laundry door across the shop. He rubbed his itching face with both hands, took in a huge breath and slowly let it go. He checked his watch.

The problem of the pickup and the bike, he thought. He'd pulled the battery from Alice's phone and tossed the phone off the bluff. He'd crisped her backpack with her iPad in the kiln after pulling that battery, too.

Never waste a good battery.

He crossed to the pickup and yanked the tarp to the floor. He placed a few pieces of lumber on the truck and re-draped the tarp so that nothing showed except tarp and concrete. He rolled his table saw against it for insurance. He wheeled Bill to the other side of the shop. Anyone who came in would focus on the Bill piece and wouldn't notice the truck. He checked his watch again, shook his head and went into the house.

Daniel hurried into the kitchen and washed his hands. He scooped a fistful of his goo out of the refrigerator and plopped it into his appliance. Again his hands trembled. Human food for days weakened him to near-fainting in the workshop. His glass filled, and Diana strolled in.

"We have a problem," he said, "and we've got to work it out now."

"You mean your girlfriend?" Diana said.

"I mean your appetite." He picked up his glass with both hands so he wouldn't slosh anything out. He drank down half and set it back under the spout to fill again and continued. "Killing for survival, that's one thing. But *this* is something else. It has to stop."

Diana shook off her sleepy-looking demeanor and took up her panther-like pacing.

"What about your precious *Jean*?" Her voice shook with anger. "*She's* a problem. She's around here too much. I don't like her in my house."

"*Our* house!" He chugged down the rest of his drink.

Diana stopped pacing to level her darkest gaze at him. She spoke in a furious whisper.

"If you want to keep her warm and full, you carry on your little dalliance at her place."

Daniel, too, rose to temper. He shoved his face right up to hers, as a dribble of blood slipped the corner of his lip.

"Don't threaten me, Sister. You, too, could be a sculpture in my new catalogue."

Her eyebrows shot up in astonishment. "You would stake me like my little pets? I think not, Brother *Dear*."

They hard-stared in silence for a heartbeat, two, close enough for a kiss. Diana reached a finger to his lip, caught the drop of blood and licked it from her finger. Daniel stepped back. Diana's expression softened.

"You don't get it," Daniel said. "You don't understand their new tools. Everybody's tracked. Even the homeless are missed. We can't have your … infections … hunting our territory, creating their own … whatever we are."

Diana stopped him with a finger to his lips. He resisted the urge to bite it off.

"Please," Diana said. "I might get bored, but I love what I am. Maybe you're a 'whatever,' but I'm an awesome creature, nearly impossible to kill."

Daniel thought, *Only nearly*. He sighed and mumbled, "And we're trapped in the dark." He checked his watch.

Diana snatched up his glass and licked it clean.

"I'll resupply tonight," he said. "My way is the only long-term answer. It's a new world. I believe it's a virus and I can beat it, eventually."

Diana made a wry face and handed back his glass. "Your pitiful drippings are survival, not satisfaction." Her voice was calm and a little slurred from her feeding. She sat at the table and leaned on an elbow, fist under her chin. She stared at the blacked-out window. "Almost dark, can you feel it?" She shifted to look him in the eye. "I hunt the old way, and that's that. You can stake them like the others, or not. I don't want to be cured, virus or not."

Daniel rinsed his glass, placed it on the drainboard, wiped his hands with a dishtowel as he tried once more for patience. Whatever came next would require calm, deliberation, a plan.

"I'll only be a couple of hours in town," he said. "If Jean comes out, don't touch her, and don't cause trouble. You and I have a lot more to discuss. Neither of us can afford to do anything stupid."

Diana turned back to the blacked-out window and said, "Exactly."

CHAPTER THIRTY-SEVEN

Jean drove Marie back to A Cut Above after their search for Alice. Her headlights illuminated James's bike leaning against the shop sign. He'd called Marie as soon as he got to Bluff Road to report she wasn't there.

"Good," Marie said. "He got back before dark."

Jean turned down the CD player that blasted "Sympathy for the Devil" to the night air. Marie opened her door but didn't get out.

Marie said, "Alice is the last person to go off on an adventure. She's never late. Never missed an appointment. Her car was home."

"And she loves that cat," Jean said. "She wouldn't leave without asking one of us to feed Rascal."

Both sat quiet for a moment, not looking at each other, brows furrowed in worry. They spoke at the same time.

"Maybe we should—?"

"Do you think we should—?"

"—call Tom?"

"—call the sheriff?"

Both voiced a nervous laugh, then quieted again. Jean turned off the CD.

"Doesn't somebody have to be missing for twenty-four hours before the law gets involved?"

Marie said, "Tom wouldn't care. Besides, it's almost twenty-four hours." She sighed. "Maybe she met somebody? She's pretty secretive about … you know."

"Alice? Where? How? She stays home, reads, and cleans the leaves of her plants with mayonnaise."

"Mayonnaise?"

Jean shrugged. "She says they like it. What do I know?"

Marie sighed again and dropped her hands to her lap. "What should we do?"

"I'm supposed to meet Daniel after he's done demonstrating goo at Brand X Beauty Parlor downtown. Maybe she showed up after I called. I don't think we should panic until morning."

Marie said, "I'm not panicked. I'm worried."

"But you're ready to panic," Jean said. "I can tell. You're all fidgety."

Marie got out, walked to the driver's side and spoke to Jean through her open window.

"I have a bad feeling, that's all. And I don't like having it. Call me when you get home. I'll call you if James knows anything."

"I may not get home tonight," Jean said. "You know why."

Marie rolled her eyes, patted Jean on the shoulder and said, "Then call me in the morning, and we'll decide what to do. If she's not back in the morning …" She shrugged.

Jean gripped Marie's hand and said, "I know. It's not her at all."

Jean started backing out, then shouted as Marie got to her door, "That girl needs a full-time mother!"

CHAPTER THIRTY-EIGHT

Tom slowly drove up the Cazador driveway with his lights on bright and window rolled down to look over the grounds as he approached. He could almost smell that this place was trouble. He didn't get a straight answer from Daniel when he asked a simple question about contractors.

If he hired Bill, and Bill did complete some work, why didn't he say something?

Instead, Tom got some blah-blah about "licensed and bonded contractors" and a vague reference to their unknown subcontractors. He'd had a long day; again he was on his own time and, technically, out of his jurisdiction and without a warrant. He stood for a moment after stepping out of his car and listened to the chorus frogs start back up. His foot slipped on a bunch of survey stakes beside the driveway. He hefted his flashlight and walked slowly to the door. He listened at the door and heard nothing but the frogs and a creaky board as he shifted his weight. He rang the bell and stepped back from the door.

A woman's voice called from inside, "Who is it?"

Tom answered in his official voice, "Sergeant Aldrich, Salish Landing Police Department."

He readied his photo ID as he heard the deadbolt unlock. The woman in the doorway was the same one he saw asleep in Cazador's truck.

"Ms. Cazador?"

"Please, come in." She opened the door wider. "Let me get the lights."

Diana turned up the dim, reddish lights, relieved that her nicks and scratches had already faded. She wore a comfortable short, white dress that accented her long legs, alabaster skin, and youthful figure. She felt her heart rate rise and used her breathing skills to settle it down.

Maybe Daniel was right, she thought. *Too much, too fast, too close to home.*

She led him to the couch and said, "Please, have a seat."

Tom remained standing and asked again, "Are you Diana Cazador?"

"Yes, I am," she said. "Is there a problem? Is my brother all right?"

"I'm Sergeant Tom Aldrich," he repeated. "I met your brother when you came to town. You were asleep." He handed Diana his ID. "As far as I know, your brother's fine."

She took a moment to study the ID, then handed it back.

"Very nice," she said. "Usually those pictures aren't any good. Like a driver's license." She reached out to shake Tom's hand and said, "Yes, my brother mentioned you were very helpful."

Tom shook her hand. "I just have some questions regarding a missing person." He hated small talk. The nervous ones loved to chat.

"Missing?" Diana asked. She tried to look like a woman afraid. "That's terrible! Out *here?*"

"About a mile from here," he said. "A car off the bluff, empty, no trace of the driver. I mentioned it to your brother. He didn't say anything?"

Diana said, "Well, he's very protective and probably didn't want to scare me, out here so far from town." She straightened and said, "Apologies, Sergeant. We have so few visitors that my manners are slipping. Can I get you something? Coffee?"

She gestured toward the couch again but Tom said, "No, thank you. Please, have a seat. I only have a couple of questions."

Diana sat on the couch, then pointed out the recliner next to it. She was careful to stifle her usual flirtatious manner. This sergeant was dangerous in ways that killing him wouldn't resolve.

"Maybe the recliner, Sergeant. All of that equipment must weigh a ton."

Tom perched on the arm of the recliner, noticed that someone had hung the Asian paintings of writing that makes pictures. The blue back-ground of the paintings was identical with the blue enamel wall, so the white Asian writing appeared as a mural. He wondered what it said.

"Yes, it does," Tom said. "You get used to it until you take it off. Now, Ms. Cazador—"

"Diana, please."

"Ms. Cazador, did Odd-Jobs Bill do any work for you out here recently?"

Diana feigned surprise.

"Bill? Why yes, he did," she said. "He put up the last of the garage siding for my brother. Daniel said he did very good work, but on his own schedule, if you know what I mean. He helped me turn this room blue. Why? Is he missing, too? Is he in trouble?"

Tom shook his head. "No, no trouble that I know of. When was the last time you saw him?"

Diana applied her best thoughtful look. "Hmm. A few days ago, at least. He came back for a tarp. I didn't see him, but the tarp is gone. I don't usually answer the door in daylight. I have a severe sun allergy."

"A few days ago ... was that Sunday, Monday?"

"Monday, I think."

"So he did the work on Friday or Saturday?"

"Maybe Sunday," she said. "Daniel would know."

"What work did he do for you?"

"Outside, mostly, the siding. But he hasn't finished the outside trim or painting. My brother does most interior work and hires exterior jobs —he shares our sun allergy. We're twins."

"Did Bill do any inside painting?

Diana shifted in her seat. This cop was zeroing in like he *knew*. Her policy about lying and keeping stories straight was never to lie about the small stuff. She sensed this was the time for the small stuff.

"Yes," she said. "He helped in this room. The exterior was Daniel's focus for him because of our allergy situation. Daniel and I can handle most of the finish work. You can see Bill does very good work when he shows up."

Tom made a bit of a show about looking at the paint job. He touched the wall.

"Enamel," he said. "Why use enamel in the living room?"

"Ah!" she said. "That was for me. I'm very fussy about clean walls for our art. We have quite a bit of art and change it often. In this case, I chose this cobalt blue to match this Mitsui collection we acquired at auction. My brother's not a slob, at all, but I'm more particular. He drags dirt in from his workshop. I like a room easy to clean. Especially since we spend most of our lives in our home."

Tom's experience was that long answers to short questions indicated someone holding back. *Why hold back about enamel?*

"Well, this room looks very nice." He stood to go. "Oh," he continued, "you said Bill left work unfinished? Do you expect him back?"

Diana stood to see him to the door. She felt his unease leak through his calm demeanor.

"I didn't have anything more for him inside," she said. "Daniel has some exterior work left, but he hasn't said when Bill would be back."

"Did he talk about family, friends?"

Diana chuckled and hoped it was disarming. "He hardly spoke at all. Just 'Yes, ma'am' and 'No, ma'am.' Very polite. I couldn't break him of the 'ma'am' habit."

"I see. Well, thanks for your time, Ms. Cazador."

Diana matched his formality. Matching people's demeanor made them more comfortable. "You're welcome here anytime, Sergeant Aldrich."

She extended her hand and Tom reciprocated. They held the handshake for a quiet moment, studying each other's eyes. Tom blinked first, and let himself out.

Tom took off his hat and tossed it into the car when a pair of headlights came down the drive. Jean pulled up beside his cruiser and stopped him.

"Tom. Tom, do you have a second?"

Diana listened intently behind the front door as Jean talked with Tom. Her hearing picked them up easily despite the door and distance.

"Sure, Jean," he said. "What's up?"

Jean got out and said, "Okay, maybe nothing. But I was going to call you in the morning."

"Call me about what?"

Jean looked up at the house and didn't see anyone at the upstairs window. She lowered her voice.

"It's Alice. She was supposed to meet James out here for a job and never showed. Very not like Alice."

Diana stepped back from the door.

Jean shut off her car and Tom asked, "She was supposed to work here, you say? When was the last time you saw her?"

"Yesterday," she said. "Out here. I brought her and James to meet Daniel. His sister has quite a lot of landscape work for them. James finished some work for them here after school, alone. Alice was supposed to bring him tools and lay out more work."

"You've probably checked her house?"

Tom was talking with Jean, but not looking at her. Now he was scanning the vicinity of the house but didn't know for what. He felt a bad tingle. He didn't want to leave Jean out there but didn't have a good reason to say so.

"Marie and I have tried to call all day. We went to her place when Marie was free. She's not home. Car's at home. Bike's gone. Cat wasn't fed, and she's crazy about that cat."

Something prickled the back of his neck.

"I'll run by there now," he said. "Where can I find you?"

"I'm meeting Daniel here for dinner. He's working late in town. I'll be here or on my boat."

Tom nudged the scatter of stakes with his toe. "He drives that new Mercedes wagon, right?"

"Yes, why?"

"He was driving out the Bluff Road when I was coming in here."

Jean rubbed her arms in the cool air. "Well, I'm early on purpose. He's demonstrating product for Marie's competition in town. I'm hoping to get on good footing with his sister. I think she's a bit jealous of his interest in me. They're twins, very close."

Tom opened his cruiser door while Jean picked up her bag and closed hers. Tom said, "Well, be careful."

Jean saw that he was serious.

"What do you mean? Careful of what?"

Tom cursed his habit of blurting and tried to cover. "You know. Of trying too hard in a relationship. Sometimes that's what kills it."

Jean laughed and slapped his shoulder. "Right. Relationship advice from the town's most dedicated bachelor. Tell it to Marie. You should marry that girl, you know."

Tom slid into the cruiser, started it up and turned on the lights. He raised his voice over the engine and spoke out his open window. "Don't consider the source. Consider the advice."

Jean waved in the headlights on her way to the house. The side door of the workshop was open slightly so she headed there instead of to the front door. Over her shoulder she said, "Whatever, Tom. You consider my advice, too!" She knew he couldn't hear but felt better for saying it.

CHAPTER THIRTY-NINE

Daniel packed several bags of red Matrix into his insulated satchel while three women in their thirties and forties reclined in salon chairs. Their eyes were closed and their breathing slow and regular. Daniel moved faster than he wanted, getting more anxious by the minute. He unpacked a tray of hot, moist towels and gently wiped their faces. One woman snored.

"Please relax and take your time before standing, you may be light in the head. Be careful of alcohol and of driving."

They all had been quiet, not at all like Marie's clients.

Maybe it was the champagne, he thought. *Maybe I should suggest it for next time.*

He didn't like rushing. He believed that conversation, his flirtatious patter, helped them relax and built a bond, an investment in long-term business. But tonight he was pressed for time. He picked up the envelope with his check, slipped it into his case, and quietly let himself out.

CHAPTER FORTY

J ean entered the side door using the flashlight on her phone and
shut the door behind her. Her beam flicked around the workshop
and stopped on the one standing sculpture. The finished product
looked cleaner, more professional on its display stand. They were fasci-
natingly ugly. She shined her light at the eye-holes. She'd thought he
would make eyes for them, but he said that would "detract from the
fright factor." She stepped closer and moved the phone so she could look
inside the eye-holes.

Snap! and the workshop flashed with light. Jean's eyes teared up while
trying to adjust to the sudden glare. "Oh!" she gasped.

Across the shop, Diana stood in the laundry room doorway wearing
black silk pajamas. Jean backed away from the sculpture.

Diana's voice was deep, commanding: "What are you doing in here?"

Jean backed farther and tripped over an electrical cord. She caught
herself on a packing crate.

"Oh, Jesus!" she blurted. "Oh, I'm sorry. I'm waiting for Daniel. I
mean, I came to start dinner for him. I thought you opened the side
door for me."

Diana didn't speak.

Jean's heart rate and breathing hit top speed. "Give me a minute to
catch my breath. You really scared me."

Diana made no move toward Jean but assessed her for a moment,
like a scientist studying a specimen.

"You want to talk. You think we should get to know each other better." Flat statements, not questions, no emotion, no tone.

Jean stammered, still trying to calm herself. "Well … I … yes, that's right."

Diana swept an arm in an exaggerated invitation into the house.

"Well, then. Come in. We'll talk."

Diana's gaze was fixed on Jean as she stepped around the sculpture and the rolls of wire toward the laundry room door. Jean felt captured in a sci-fi tractor beam that pulled her forward. She wanted to get along, be nice, do the right thing. Jean reached the doorway, and Diana took her by the hand to lead her inside to the stairway to her room.

"Set your things here," Diana said, indicating a small parlor table.

Jean left her purse and jacket, then followed Diana up the stairs. The cold from Diana's hand remained. Dim red lights cast bloody shadows in the dark blue living room. Diana's room was black. Completely black—walls and ceiling—except for the hardwood floor. A single red nightlight beside the bed revealed a huge bedroom half-filled with barbells, treadmill, stepper, stationary bike. A slick drop cloth covered the king-sized bed and most of the floor. Jean stood in the doorway.

Diana heard Jean's breathing and pulse, smelled … apprehension, not quite fear.

"Come here."

Jean said, "But I …"

"Come inside. Close the door. I will explain everything."

A voice, Tom's voice, whispered in Jean's head, "Be careful." She considered entering the room, then took a step back.

Diana attacked in a blinding rush. She pinned Jean against the hallway wall with a smothering grip on her trachea. Jean uttered a few squeaks through her tight throat and thrashed wildly at Diana, with no effect. Diana clamped her other hand over Jean's nose and mouth. Jean fought clumsily, furiously, but ran out of air quickly and slumped to the floor. Diana didn't stop to feed.

"Something special for you, sister," she whispered.

Diana dragged her across the threshold and into her room, then wrestled her onto the bed. From the bedstand, under the red nightlight, she picked up her mother's ivory-handled tool, and flicked open the blade.

"Let's not make a huge mess," she said. "Brother Dear has an important decision to make."

CHAPTER FORTY-ONE

D aniel saw Jean's old Chevy in the driveway and didn't even shut the garage door after pulling inside. He grabbed his satchel, jumped out of the car, and nearly tripped over his trough full of sculpture material, ready to mix. A roll of chicken wire lay alongside.

"Diana!"

In the living room, he saw Jean's bag and coat atop the side table. He glanced around the room, then sniffed the air. He felt his stomach drop.

"Shit!"

He clambered up the stairs and slammed open Diana's door. Diana and Jean lay in the dim red light side-by-side on Diana's bed. The night-light revealed a small black pool of blood next to Jean's neck, and a smear across Diana's nose, mouth, chin. Diana's head lolled back on her pillow, her eyes heavy-lidded, barely open.

Daniel felt for Jean's unwounded carotid, hoping, hoping.

There!

Thin and thready but there, and none of the usual ripping, tearing, shredding Diana preferred. The wound on the other side opened that carotid vertically about two inches, its edges pale and puckered. Diana stirred, lifted her head without opening her eyes.

"Must be the salt air," she murmured. "I've been ravenous."

Daniel ignored her. He stroked Jean's hair, bent down and kissed her forehead. His fingers trembled with fear, anger, rage.

Diana propped herself up on her elbows and opened her eyes. They weren't tracking well.

"I've done the thing you couldn't do for yourself," she said. She grunted, and fell back onto her pillow. "Now you have each other. Forever." She picked up Jean's limp hand. "We can be family, now, of a sort."

Her deep breathing always preceded her post-feeding slide into oblivion. She roused, opened her eyes and whispered, "Of course, you could stake her like the others. It's up to you." She snuggled against Jean and began the fall into torpor.

Daniel calculated what needed to be done, and whether he had time to get to storage in Port Angeles and retrieve the truck containing his backup electronics. He checked his phone for the ferry to Canada and felt his stomach go cold.

Only two runs a day. Both in daylight!

Darkest Knight had forgotten, or disregarded, their most important requirement for safety—night passage. And Daniel hadn't double-checked.

"All the other ferries run most of the night!" he told himself. He'd made assumptions. "Careless!" he snapped.

Now Daniel was grateful for the instinct that had urged him to take one complete set of backup IDs to Salish Landing with him.

Time to get creative!

He opened their passports, checked the photos provided by Darkest Knight, and found them both passable. Darkest Knight had followed his description of the necessary stand-ins to the letter. He'd been most worried about Diana's, but it was better than he'd hoped for.

Daniel stuffed his protective gear into his bug-out bag with his cedar puzzle-box of Canadian IDs and credit cards. He gathered up the bag, his satchel of Matrix and his appliance and put them into the back of Bill's pickup. He lifted a gas can out of the back of the pickup and set it on the workshop floor. He started Bill's truck, pulled it into the driveway and stepped onto the pile of survey stakes. He selected a stake and stuck it into the back of his belt, then he drove Jean's car into the garage and parked it next to his Mercedes. He used his cutting torch to remove Bill from his pedestal and dragged him through the laundry door and into the house where he wrestled it onto the couch. He hurried back to the workshop to grab his short-handled sledgehammer and the gas can, then hustled them up the stairs and into the bedroom.

He gripped the survey stake in a trembling fist and moved the body to place the tip correctly.

Diana mumbled, "Brother Dear, family?"

Daniel slammed the hammer onto the top of the stake. A grunt, the wet suck of a chest wound in the final struggle, a wheeze. Daniel lifted Jean's body and navigated the stairs without falling. He carried her out to the driveway and laid her across the passenger seat of Bill's pickup. He hurried back to the workshop and fumbled through his tool chest for the wrench for the propane line. He ran back up the stairs and used the gas can to wet down the body on the bed, the sculpture on the couch, his clean room, a trail of gas to his car in the garage. He opened the gas caps to both cars.

Daniel disconnected the propane line behind the laundry room door. He pulled the garage door almost down, scratched a spark from his welding lighter and ducked the hot flash under the door. He yanked it down all the way and ran to Bill's truck. Already he could see a fire-flash through the upstairs window. Daniel started the truck and raced the old rattletrap down the driveway to beat the failure of that propane tank. He made the highway just as Odd-Job Bill's rearview mirror lit up. A propane fireball boiled above the treetops.

CHAPTER FORTY-TWO

Tom met Sid, the local department's fire investigator, at the Bluff Road property. He'd directed traffic and handled incident security in his street clothes until a deputy showed up to take charge for the county. Tom and Sid sat on the rear running board of the #5 pumper, sipped hot black coffee, and stared at the smoke, steam, and blackened rubble of Casa Cazador. A young volunteer firefighter, a senior cheerleader at James's school, limped toward the truck, humping a roll of scorched hose line.

Sid asked, "How'd you get that limp?"

She stepped onto the running board beside them and grunted the roll up to the hose bed.

"That second floor," she said. "We couldn't get up there. Captain said, 'Stand back, let it burn.' Everything twisted when the second floor dropped, got the side of my knee. Did they tell you about the second victim?"

Both Tom and Sid stood up. "No," Sid said. He set his coffee down. "Tell me. Weird, like the first one?"

Her long, black hair was singed at the ends that poked out from under her helmet. Tom tried to remember her name ... Stephanie. Her eyes were red and swollen from the smoke and ash, and her lips quivered. She covered her mouth.

"Breathe," Sid said. "Deep breaths."

"She fell on me!" Stephanie blurted, then talked fast. "She wasn't hard-skinned like the gross one downstairs. Some of her smeared on my gear. Randy hosed her off me. She was a she, all burned up with a piece of wood through her chest."

Sid waved over an EMT from the aid car idling up the driveway. He shook Stephanie's hand. "Good job, Rookie," he said. "Let these guys look at the knee. They'll take you to the ER to check you out. Department insurance covers you."

Sid's portable radio squawked, "Got a third crispy critter. This one in a box!"

Sid keyed his mike and in an even voice said, "Reporting party, that is a *deceased person*. Have some respect, asshole!"

Tom imagined applause in all living rooms in the county with scanners. He set his cold, unfinished coffee next to Sid's. "All boxed up," he told Sid. "How convenient. Shall we?"

Sid made a show of holstering his radio. "I'll hear about *that* tomorrow."

The EMTs had all three bodies laid out between two tarps alongside what was left of the garage. Tom recognized Daniel's Mercedes, but he took a moment to realize that the burned-up Chevy beside it was Jean's. His heart kicked into high gear.

Shit! he thought. "This is Jean's car, Sid. Marie's friend?"

"Shit!" Sid said. "Fuck!"

An EMT pulled away the top tarp, and Tom caught his breath. No way he could tell whether the woman victim was Jean or Diana.

Or someone else? he wondered. Whether the hair had been blonde-ish or reddish, it was a melted, peeling lump of black now. Sid tilted the body to reveal her back, and Tom saw the pointed end of a survey stake. He walked back up the driveway and found the scatter of stakes. He picked one up by the tip and asked a firefighter, "Could you cover these for me? They may be evidence." He placed the stake into a plastic bag from the aid car and headed back to Sid.

Tom let Sid finish his preliminaries and tried to stay upwind. The other two bodies didn't look real. Hard material, jagged edges like a bad plaster job, cocooned them.

"He's a sculptor," he called to Sid. "Are those people? Or things?"

"Things on the outside," Sid called back. "Can't tell about the insides."

"I have some questions," Tom said.

"I'll bet you have."

Sid folded his notebook and shot a few more pictures with his cell.

The department's field photographer took over, and Sid joined Tom back at the truck.

Sid showed Tom his photos, starting with the woman. "Foreign object, wood, through-and-through. Must've been a helluva blast." Next photo was a thing. "Also foreign object, cut off at both ends, covered with this shell." Next photo. "Through the eye-holes, with the flash, you can see the object."

Tom stopped him and enlarged the picture. "What was all that metal in there? What kind of blast does *that*?"

"Right," Sid said. "Goes to your 'thing' theory. But see *that* and *that* in there? Burned tissue."

The lumps that Sid pointed out looked like burned residue in the bottom of an oven, flecked with splinters of scorched china.

"Bone," Sid said, anticipating a question. "Pretty sure. So, what's your theory about the foreign objects, Mr. Spock? Spears?"

Tom shook his head and led Sid around the front of the truck to the survey stakes, now covered with clear plastic, secured at the corners with rocks.

"Spock always said 'theory,'" Tom said. "He meant 'hypothesis.' I got it wrong on a science test because of him."

"Hmm. Very short spears. Close quarters, indeed. What about the one in the box?" Sid called up the photo. "People hide in strange places in fire."

Tom enlarged the shot and pointed to the half-burned lid, nailed at the edges. "Thing or not," he said, "it didn't crawl in there and nail the top down after itself."

The wind shifted onshore and carried the oily odor of death right to their faces. Sid and Tom turned their backs, and Sid pulled two cigars from his coat pocket. He lit Tom's, then his own. They each puffed to get them going.

Sid waved his cigar and said, "Only thing I've found to cut the smell." He puff-puffed a fog of smoke around his head. "It's gonna take some lab work for this one, maybe a week for that. X-rays we can do today. This torch knows his chemistry. Owners?"

"Brother and sister," Tom said. His eyes watered from the cigar smoke and the pervasive stink off the tarp. "We have some missing people. Marie said Alice the landscaper's been missing since yesterday. Now, maybe Jean." Tom hoped he wasn't smelling what was left of Jean but didn't say anything. He was over being shocked and moved right into being pissed.

"Maybe it's the sister."

"Can't tell, like you said. Two women missing. That's what's left of Jean's car next to what's left of her new boyfriend's car in what's left of the garage. I saw her last night in this driveway. I had a bad feeling about the sister. The sister's unaccounted for until we get IDs." Tom counted on his fingers. "Three women. Three bodies, but only one of them female. If one of the things is the brother, who's the other? We can't even tell for sure if bodies are in those shells. Shit."

Sid rubbed his chin. "We'll have to wait for DNA to find out who, or what." He paused. "This is not a good time for friends of Marie. Maybe somebody's after *you*."

Tom turned his head, took a furtive swipe at his eyes, puffed hard on his cigar. His stomach reminded him that he didn't smoke. He had to admit, it helped with the smell. He shook his head. "Don't think so. Everything about this pair is a mystery."

"Jealous ex?" Sid asked.

Tom spat a chunk of cigar off his lip and worked on his professional composure. "Who knows?" he said. "Marie says the guy's a player. Crime lab should be here in the morning. Maybe they'll have something." He waved a hand at the scene. "Lots of ugly detail to sift through."

"Got news for you, Aldrich," Sid said. "It's already morning. Great, there's the coroner with body bags. Hope the two hardshells fit."

Tom looked east where the tip of the sun topped the shoulder of Mt. Rainier and cast an inverted shadow across a patch of gray clouds at the top. He spit again and crushed the cigar out in the gravel.

"I need my preliminary typed up before they get here. Meeting's at 0900. They'll want your report, too."

Sid grumped, "They'll have it when *I* have it! This is a bad one. I'm not wasting anybody's time on assumptions!"

A shout from behind: "Hey! Hey there!"

The Coroner held up the covering tarp and pointed at steam rising from the female corpse. The crusty black surface began to bubble. "Sid! Aldrich!" He uncovered the bodies completely and a flicker of flame licked a crack in the crust.

"Jesus!" Sid said. "Never seen anything like that." He turned to the firefighters and shouted, "Get some foam on this one *now*! No extinguishers, we don't know the chemistry here."

The woman's body continued to bubble and spilled a sheet of blue flame as the bubbles burst. The firefighters smothered the body with at least a foot of foam before the fire action settled down.

The Coroner stood back, wide-eyed and stunned. He and his assistant laid the body bags next to the tarps.

"I'm not hauling that one in *my* rig," the Coroner said.

Sid took a deep breath, coughed, and said, "Bag her up. We'll haul her in a pickup, just in case. Jesus!" He turned to Tom. "We need to find out what the hell this guy used."

"You do that," Tom said. "I need to find the guy."

Already Tom was walking the driveway up to his car. He felt like shit from the cigar smoke on top of the other smoke and grit he'd been eating all night. He had no experience to process what he'd just seen. Not much scared him, but this one did.

He parked at the foot of City Dock beside the station. He stepped out of the cruiser as sunrise swept across the bay and bedazzled the wavetops at the tideline. A buzzing sound emerged from behind the station, the small engine of a sailboat making very slow time toward the Strait. A light wind flapped the station's flag overhead.

Perfect day for sailing, Tom thought. He yawned, rubbed his face and leaned across the hood of his car. *But they're not sailing. Crawling along instead.*

Tom reached into the car for his clipboard, radio, and phone. He unlocked the door to the station, closed the door, and stopped cold.

A perfect day for sailing, he thought. *Jean has a liveaboard.*

He threw his clipboard and notes onto the desk and yanked a bottom drawer all the way out, spilling everything onto the floor. He snatched up his binoculars and stumbled on the drawer as he raced out the door to the end of City Dock.

He swept the bay in careful passes and calmed his breathing to steady the view. A blurry image. Back. The deck of a sailboat, no one in sight. He fine-focused on a boathook from the cabin hatch below to the tiller above. He focused on the stern with the name:

"*Freedom*
Salish Landing WA"

in vivid pink letters.

"Shit shit shit!"

Tom pulled out his cell and speed dialed his brother. *Please be gearing up today!*

Mark said, "Speak, my brother! Tell me you're fishing today!"

"Get *Fishkiller* to the City Dock pronto," Tom said. "Emergency. Will fill you in."

He hung up as soon as his brother said, "Sure, hey …" He picked up his portable and keyed the mike on his run back to the office for a rifle.

"Dispatch, 16 portable."

"Go ahead, 16."

"Request assistance intercepting sailing vessel *Freedom* heading for the Strait. Does county have their speedboat available?"

Tom was breathing hard when he reached the rifle rack.

"Negative," Dispatch said. "Boat and dive team are in Seattle for re-cert."

He fumbled the round security key into the lock and grabbed a rifle and two loaded clips.

"Request all-agency alert, with Coast Guard and reserves with boats." He spoke on the run, out of breath, and hoped he didn't move out of radio range. He clicked the portable twice for reply.

"Received, 16. Time 0745."

His brother powered full-speed toward him a hundred yards out. Tom continued, "I'm in pursuit in yellow fishboat *Fishkiller*. Homicide and arson suspect on board sailboat *Freedom*, possible kidnapping in progress, consider armed and dangerous. 16 out."

Mark roared in hot, swung his boat around and banged the pier as Tom leapt aboard. Mark glanced at the rifle and said, "*Hunting* salmon now?"

They took a pounding as Mark wound out his Chrysler Six through the chop in the channel and the wind. Tom couldn't focus on detail through the glasses and cursed the shooting conditions. In spite of the *slam slam slam* of the boat, he caught a glimpse of a gloved hand and an arm heavily swathed in sailcloth maneuvering the tiller from below.

CHAPTER FORTY-THREE

Jean woke in the forward berth of *Freedom* with a heavy gauze bandage tight to her neck. She felt woozy, weak, and disoriented. *Home on* Freedom, she realized. *Was it a nightmare?* She felt no pain, but something itched her neck. She reached a hand up and found the bandage.

"Oh, fuck!" She felt ice in her belly and lifted her head. Daniel lay at the other end of the passageway, bundled into his sun protection augmented with a space blanket cover. He operated the tiller with a boathook duct-taped to his right hand. He glanced back at her, and his mask and welder's goggles looked starkly alien.

Definitely alien.

He sprawled atop a pile of her charts and focused on something in his hand.

Compass, she thought. She felt no pain except terror. *What are they? What have they done?*

All the portholes were blacked out with duct tape. The steady yammer wasn't just the engine. Daniel had been talking through the engine noise and her fog, but now Jean could understand.

"We can make a life up there, you'll see."

He wasn't looking at her. She watched him over her bare feet that pointed to him in the stern. His feet with his expensive Italian shoes lay toward the bow, two or three steps from hers. Her own breathing felt unusually good, like she'd held her breath for a week, but it sounded loud to her so she forced some control.

"We're smart people," he was saying, "we don't have to hurt anyone. My sister … Ah!" He yanked his hand farther into the cabin. His sleeve pulled back from his glove and pink bubbles dotted his wrist. He pulled the sleeve down, stripped some duct tape from a roll with his teeth, and covered the gap. He laughed the bad-guy laugh she always hated in the movies.

Jesus! They actually laugh like that!

Jean felt herself getting stronger and scanned for weapons. The knife rack in the galley was too close to Daniel, as was the coil of line at his feet.

Will a knife even work with them, whatever they are?

"We heal fast—you already feel that, don't you?" he said. "You'll need to eat, soon, to complete the change."

The locker at Jean's feet held her fire extinguisher and her orange emergency flare kit.

Daniel stiffened, let go the boathook and scooted farther into the cabin.

"They're coming!" he announced. His face and eyes weren't visible, but the frantic swiveling of his head betrayed his panic.

So, they feel fear!

Jean felt a spurt of confidence at the thought. She sat up, immediately started to gag, and placed her head between her knees. The deck hatch to the engine room lay right at her feet. A bigger engine growled over the whine of her own and something big *bang bang bang*ed over the wave chop. She caught her breath while Daniel cowered behind the cabin bulkhead, not looking her way. She eased open the hatch to the engine and stopped to see whether he noticed the change in sound. He wriggled around, trying to get a safe look at whoever approached.

Jean scanned the electrical system, fuel hardware, plumbing, and two sea valves attached to the hull. She set the hatch cover aside, opened her locker, and snatched up the orange flare case. The sudden movement exhausted her. She lay back down and covered the case to muffle the snap when she opened it.

She heard the crackled garble of a bullhorn nearby.

"Freedom!" it shouted. "This is Sergeant Aldrich, Salish Landing Police! Throttle back and come around!"

Daniel maintained his speed and course. He looked exhausted or weak from the sun.

Jean loaded the 12-gauge flare gun with shaking hands.

White, she thought. *White should do it.* She clicked the breech shut and didn't feel afraid anymore. An understanding flooded through her, that her body was something different now, that she couldn't be saved. But she had a mission. A refreshing calm washed over her.

Her resolve hardened when her feet started to burn from the slit of sunlight through the hatchway to the helm. She yanked them back and pulled her knees tight to her chest.

It's not an allergy at all, you lying shit!

The sheet that she flipped over her feet hurt, too, and when she rubbed the burn she came away with mushy skin. She breathed deep a couple of times and affirmed her decision.

"Freedom!" from the bullhorn. "Cut your engine and come around. Prepare for boarding."

Jean leaned halfway into the engine hatch and opened both sea valves. Sea water gushed in through both ports, and Daniel still concentrated on the approaching boat. The engine would die in a few minutes.

Daniel hollered back at Jean, "Don't worry, I can destroy them if they board us. I'm not like my sister, but I *can* save us!"

You look finished to me, Jean thought.

Jean pulled herself to a sitting position, flare gun in her right hand. She gripped a second shell in her left. She ran her hand over the mahogany trim around her berth, recalled the dark-haired lover who made it and the light-haired lover who forged the ornate bronze fittings on her hatch cover.

She sucked in a big breath and hollered as loud as she could, "Tom! Tom Aldrich!"

The approaching boat's engine throttled back. Daniel dropped the boathook and turned to see Jean, the flare gun, and the water splashing up from below decks.

"What are you doing? I can handle this! He can't hear over the engines." He reached toward her.

Their own engine cut out and Jean smelled fuel on the water. The oncoming boat cut its engine for contact.

"Tom Aldrich! Tom!"

The kick from her flare gun nearly knocked it from her hand. Her white flare caught Daniel square in the chest. It burned and burrowed its way through his space blanket and layers of clothes. He tried to scrabble it away, but the burning material stuck and continued through the gloves to his hands. He thrashed against the boathook and dislodged the hatch cover to the deck. The cabin flashed with sunlight, and he snapped into a fetal position.

The glare blinded Jean and her skin seared all over. She loaded the flare gun by feel and aimed for the engine room and the fuel rising atop the water. Daniel started unintelligible screaming as he scuttled back from the light and closer to her.

She felt the familiar *bump bump bump* of another vessel coming alongside. This time she hollered, "Get back, Tom! Take care of Marie!"

Tom heard Jean and the agonized screams from below.

Mark held *Fishkiller* fast to *Freedom*.

"She's riding low!" Mark shouted at Tom. "Taking on water!"

Jean aimed the flare gun at the engine. "Red," she said, and fired.

The red flash overtook the white flare, and the ignited fuel *whooshed* throughout the cabin.

Tom wished he'd grabbed his sidearm. He tossed his bulky rifle aside, grabbed the safety rail, and fought to control his sea legs. He leapt onto *Freedom* just as her cabin exploded in a hot, red flash.

CHAPTER FORTY-FOUR

Tom heard beeping and radio static and reached for his portable, but he couldn't move. He couldn't feel anything, either, and his vision was cockeyed. All he could see was a white ceiling with all kinds of hardware hanging from it. He managed to lift his head enough to see his right arm and hand bulked up with bandages and secured to a board attached to the bed. His left arm had an IV drip going, also secured to a board. Wires for telemetry stuck to his chest. His nose itched.

Hospital, he thought. *Hunh.*

The right side of his head felt cold when he rubbed it on his pillow. The other side tickled and felt crusty. He turned to the crusty side and saw Marie asleep in a plastic chair next to the bed. He remembered the boat, the flash …

"Jean!" he blurted. His throat felt raw and he didn't recognize his voice. His head hurt now, and his face felt sunburned.

Marie startled awake and leaned over him, her brow furrowed and her eyes red.

"Hello, Tom." She gripped his left hand.

His raw throat managed, "Hello, Marie." He had to swallow and couldn't. Marie put a straw to his lips and he sucked up fresh, cold, soothing water. He stopped to catch his breath and croaked, "Mark? Is my brother okay?"

"He's okay," she said. "He went home the first night. Burns on his arm and hand, cuts on his back. The Coast Guard was right behind you and fished both of you out."

"Fishkiller?" he rasped.

"Still afloat," she said. "Coast Guard Auxiliary towed it in." Marie checked her watch. "Almost seven," she said. "Mark's usually here by 7:30."

Tom let "the first night" and "usually here" sink in.

"How long have I been here?"

"At about 10:30 it'll be three days," she said.

"Three days!" Tom struggled to sit up with the IV lines, blood pressure cuff, cardiac monitor leads and his first glimmer of real pain. He fell back in a sweat.

"How long do I *have* to be here?"

Marie's gaze didn't meet his.

"You're awake, that's the big thing," she said. "The doc says he'll know more when you can talk."

"Which doc?"

"Doc Rowe," she said. "He said he ran track against you in high school."

"Not against me," Tom said. "Against our team. He ran hurdles. I preferred races without crap in the way."

Tom felt restless in spite of the pain and worked himself back to a sitting position. The boards attached to his arms made it a struggle, and he panted with the effort. That started coughing in his raw throat.

Marie stuffed extra pillows behind his back. "Sorry, I don't know how to put the bed up," she said. "The nurse will get it."

"When?" He regretted sounding irritated even though he was. If they had anything to give him for all this burning, he was ready.

"They make rounds at seven," Marie said. "I'll have to go by ten. We're having a memorial for Jean and Alice and Odd-Jobs Bill at the park. I'm glad it's not for you."

"Me, too," Tom said. "All three of them? I knew something was screwy. I'm really sorry about Jean and Alice. Bill, too. I had a bad feeling—"

Marie shook her head. "From what I hear, nobody would've guessed what was going on out there."

"I'm *paid* to guess," he said, "and paid to guess *right*. What the hell *was* going on? Anybody know, yet?"

"No," she said, "not yet." She squeezed his good hand too tight. "Stop thinking about it. Concentrate on getting out of here. By the way, Doc Rowe says that when he lets you out you can't be alone for a few days."

Tom started to protest. "But I don't—"

Marie put a finger to her lips to shush him. "That was a hint, Tom. Move in with us while you get better. The kids voted 'yes.' Both of them."

Tom's heart monitor picked up its beep.

"Jean," he started, then swallowed hard. He sighed and started again. "Sorry. All I remember when we got to her boat was a flash—two flashes. Between them Jean yelled, 'Take care of Marie!' Her last words."

Neither of them blinked nor breathed for a moment. Tom's monitor picked up speed again, and he squeezed her hand back.

"Marie?" he wheezed. "Will you marry me?"

Marie teared up and said, "Oh, Tom, you have a head injury. Maybe you're not in your right mind."

He smiled and said, "Well, then, this would be your opportunity if you wanted to snag it ... me."

"Okay," she said, "but no intensive care bedside vows. We'll have to clean you up first."

"So 'okay' is a 'yes'?"

Marie kissed his forehead. "Yes, Tom, it's a 'yes.'"

Doc Rowe and Nurse Kasey pushed back the curtain, and Kasey winked at Marie, tilted her head towards Tom and raised her eyebrows in a question.

Marie cleared her throat, placed her hands on her belly, looked Tom straight in the eye and said, "Oh, by the way, Tom. That morning sickness wasn't the garlic."

CHAPTER FORTY-FIVE

Lucy taped a hand-lettered sign over the logo on her mom's shop door that read,
"Closed for Honeymoon!
Sunshine or Bust!"

Below that she taped a picture of the wedding party. In the photo, Tom had some recovery to go. His stitches were out but the fresh scars remained a vivid, angry red. He sported his first mohawk because most of his hair was melted off on the left. Bleached hair tips made the stubbly top shimmer like a crest on a proud bird. Lucy stared open-mouthed at Tom's haircut and mimed astonishment. James smiled wide and held a large silver cross between his teeth. Tom smiled down at Marie from behind, and she gazed up at him. His scarred hands interlaced with hers across her belly, and her diamond ring dazzled in the sun.

ACKNOWLEDGMENTS

Many thanks to Kevin J. Anderson, Rebecca Moesta, and Sarah Hoyt for this opportunity! Thanks for support from Mark Mandell, Nancy Holder, and Anna Quinn/The Writer's Workshoppe! Also a nod to granddaughter Nathalie Johnson, for detail on hair salons.

ABOUT THE AUTHOR

Bill Ransom is the coauthor with Frank Herbert of the best-selling Pandora Sequence: *The Jesus Incident, The Lazarus Effect,* and *The Ascension Factor.* He has also written three gritty, solo science fiction novels, *Jaguar, ViraVax,* and *Burn.*

An accomplished poet, Ransom pioneered the National Endowment for the Arts' Poetry in the Schools program in Washington and in several western states. He founded and directed the popular Port Townsend Writers' Conference and Youth Programs for Centrum. His collection, *Finding True North & Critter* was nominated for both the Pulitzer Prize and the National Book Award in poetry.

Ransom appeared in two feature films: *An Officer and a Gentleman* and *The Caine Mutiny Court-Martial* (CBS). He was a jet engine expeditor, cook, framer, and roofer; firefighter, firefighting basic training instructor, and CPR instructor for six years; an Advanced Life Support Emergency Medical Technician for ten years in Washington and with humanitarian medical groups in civil wars in Guatemala, El Salvador, and Nicaragua. He's had plenty of experience with blood.

Brother Blood, Sister Death is his seventh novel.

IF YOU LIKED ...

IF YOU LIKED BROTHER BLOOD, SISTER DEATH, YOU
MIGHT ALSO ENJOY:

ViraVax
by Bill Ransom

Jaguar
by Bill Ransom

Band on the Run
by D.J. Butler

OTHER WORDFIRE PRESS TITLES BY BILL RANSOM

Burn

Jaguar

Vira Vax

Our list of other WordFire Press authors and titles is always growing. To find out more and to see our selection of titles, visit us at:
wordfirepress.com

www.ingramcontent.com/pod-product-compliance
Lightning Source LLC
Chambersburg PA
CBHW050142110726
47898CB00008B/2639